SHOCK TOTEM
PUBLICATIONS

PUBLISHER/EDITOR
K. Allen Wood

CONTRIBUTING EDITORS
John Boden
Catherine Grant
Barry Lee Dejasu
Zachary C. Parker

COPY EDITOR
Sarah Gomes

LAYOUT/DESIGN
K. Allen Wood

COVER DESIGN
Mikio Murakami

Established in 2009
www.shocktotem.com

Copyright © 2014 by Shock Totem Publications, LLC.

All rights reserved. No part of this publication may be reproduced or transmitted in any form, including photocopying, recording or by any information storage and retrieval system, without the written consent of Shock Totem Publications, LLC, except where permitted by law.

The short stories in this publication are works of fiction. Names, characters, places, and incidents either are the product of the author's imagination or are used fictitiously. Any resemblance to actual persons, living or dead, events, or locales is entirely coincidental. The views expressed in the nonfiction writing herein are solely those of the authors.

ISSN 1944-110X

Printed in the United States of America.

Notes from the Editor's Desk

Welcome to issue #8!

If there were ever an issue to test my resolve, it was this one. Each issue presents challenges, like the order in which to put the stories, making sure everyone contributes their reviews, bios, story notes on time—you know, typical publisher stuff. But this time things were different...

There was a baby in the house.

Any parent will tell you raising children is a lot of work. This is something all non-parents take for granted, I think, because "a lot of work" is an understatement. Sleep deprivation is a serious problem, which makes editing and writing a daunting task. Free time is spent napping. Holding a baby requires at least one arm, so that makes typing nearly impossible. The list goes on.

My wife and I have a wonderful little boy, who smiles all the time and rarely cries. Blessed, in a word. Lucky, in another. Had we a colicky baby, I'm not sure this issue (or the three other books I put together in the last four months) would ever have come out.

But I wouldn't change any of it. Not a single second. And though a tad late, *Shock Totem #8* is here—*behold!*—and I think it's a fantastic issue. Which probably surprises no one.

But let's see, we've got **Cody Goodfellow** and **John Skipp**, who as collaborators have penned numerous short stories as well as the modern-horror classics *Jake's Wake* and *Spore*. Here, however, they both provide individual stories—"The Barham Offramp Playhouse" and "Depresso the Clown," respectively—for your reading pleasure.

Carlie St. George's "We Share the Dark" follows a woman struggling to leave her ghosts behind. "Death and the Maiden," by **David Barber**, revisits a classic time and a classic character in horror fiction. **D.A. D'Amico's** "Watchtower" and **John C. Foster's** "Highballing Through Gehenna" both traverse surreal landscapes full of monsters and madness.

WC Roberts, last seen in our third issue, returns with another mindbending slice of poetry.

Newcomer **Harry Baker** honors us with his first sale, "Fat Betty," a stark reminder that sometimes it's better to give than to take. "Stabat Mater," by **Michael Wehunt**, was our flash fiction contest winner for 2013, chosen by our guest judge, **Bracken MacLeod**, as the best of the five bi-monthly winning stories for the year.

In addition to all the fiction-y goodness, you will find conversations with **Cody Goodfellow** and rising star **Adam Cesare**, narrative nonfiction by **Catherine Grant**, an article by **Joe Modzelewski**, reviews, and more...

So there you have it. All the sleepless nights—or days in my case—may have made this issue a much more difficult undertaking than past issues, but when all is said and done, I think this is another fine issue. I can only hope you do as well.

And say, if this isn't enough for you, right on its heels comes our Valentine's Day issue, the second in our ongoing series of holiday releases. If you're looking for a collection of "love" stories, we've got you covered.

As always, take care and stay well.

K. Allen Wood
January 1, 2014

Contents

Nosferatu: The Origin of Vampires on Screen: An Article
by Joe Modzelewski 7

Highballing Through Gehenna
by John C. Foster 9

We Share the Dark
by Carlie St. George 23

The Highland Lord Brought Low: Narrative Nonfiction
by Catherine Grant 35

Swearing at the Dinner Table: A Conversation with Cody Goodfellow
by John Boden 41

The Barham Offramp Playhouse
by Cody Goodfellow 49

Whisperings Sung Through the Neighborhood of Stilted Sorrows
by WC Roberts 61

Strange Goods and Other Oddities 65

Watchtower
by D.A. D'Amico 75

Death and the Maiden
by David Barber 81

Bloodstains & Blue Suede Shoes, Part 6
by John Boden and Simon Marshall-Jones 87

Fat Betty
by Harry Baker 91

Until I'm Dead: A Conversation with Adam Cesare
by John Boden 101

Stabat Mater: 2013 Shock Totem Flash Fiction Contest Winner
by Michael Wehunt 109

Depresso the Clown
by John Skipp 113

Howling Through the Keyhole 119

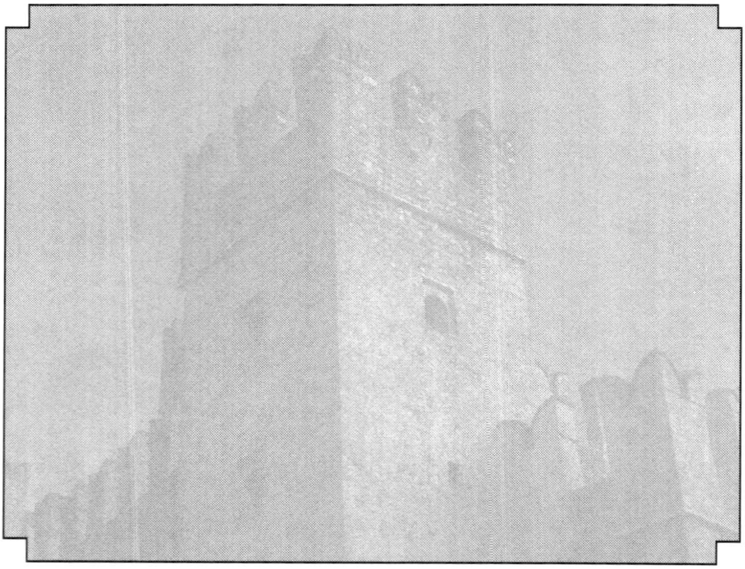

Article
NOSFERATU: THE ORIGIN OF VAMPIRES ON SCREEN

by Joe Modzelewski

In recent years, the modern vampire has flooded our pop-culture zeitgeist. From TV shows such as *Vampire Diaries* or *True Blood* to recent movies such as the infamous *Twilight* series or even *Abraham Lincoln: Vampire Hunter*, which showcases a presidential icon combating monsters colonial style, it seems that the modern horror archetype of the vampire has seeped its way into nearly every nook and cranny of the entertainment medium.

It appears that our world will always be engrossed with blood-sucking, neck-biting creatures of the night. However, it was not always so that vampires could have love-interests with mere mortals or that they held even the slightest bit of romantic or likeable attraction. There was a time where vampires were seen as strictly terrifying demons that would make your spine tingle with fear at just the thought. On film, the classic vampire came into fruition with a 1922 German film, *Nosferatu*.

The presence of vampire-like creatures in folklore and mythology dates back to ancient civilizations. However, the actual term "vampire" was first recorded in the English language in the mid-18th century. Back then, it was spelled vampyre; but in the past century or so that has changed to how it is commonly spelled today. Vampire legend was once very popular in rural Eastern European countries and many tales were derived from alleged experiences and confrontations with supposed vampire-like beings. Some accused were tried and put on trial for the possibility of being a vampire.

The romanticised, gaunt, pale, eerily charming vampire that we all are familiar with today did not entirely exist until 1897, with Bram Stoker's *Dracula*. This would become known as the definitive work of fiction in regard to what exactly a vampire is. Its influence would ring true for decades and even a century later. Although there were other literary takes on vampires before it, *Dracula* became the most highly regarded and revered.

At the time as the success of *Dracula*, film and the concept of cinema was quickly gaining attraction. This was especially true in Europe. It is even said that at one time (and still argued today) that European cinema was much more advanced and beyond its time than Hollywood ever was in North America. German and French filmmakers were leading the way in film innovation. German director F.W. Marnau felt that *Dracula* would make a wonderful screen adaptation. Of course this would be true for decades to come, as countless takes on the stories have been made, but it was a ambitious project for the time.

Marnau was unable to obtain the legal rights to Dracula, and so while he still used it as basis of the plot, he changed a few details to avoid being a direct copy. Dracula was changed to Nosferatu, Count Dracula was changed to Count Orlok, Jonathan Harker to Thomas Hutter, Mina Harker to Ellen Hutter, and so on. Some plot points were changed, but the product is something that can truly stand on its own and still to this day holds up as an irresistibly creepy and haunting tale of suspense and horror.

Nosferatu, released in 1922, is credited with being the first vampire film ever made and at the time, it really shocked and scared audiences. Its full title, *Nosferatu: A Symphony of Horror*, is true to the film itself. Although silent, the beautiful score that is played throughout, originally composed by Hans Erdmann, effortlessly sets the tones of each scene with a flux that changes from serene fluidity to jagged terror. The music allows each shot to evoke such genuine emotions from the audience that are not purely nostalgic but contemporary and real.

Each scene in *Nosferatu* displays a certain tint for whatever time of day it is and each shade of color adds to the simple black and white, which on its own can be quite powerful as well. *Nosferatu* is a haunting film on its own merit, but a true standout performance is made by Max Schreck, who plays as Count Orlok. Schreck is sure to strike a certain discomfort with his hollowed eyes and ghostly appeal. The way he stares out at the audience, vacant yet menacing and, amidst the absence of sound, unnerving. The lack of any sort of sound besides the composed score gives you the sense of a nightmarish realm of twisted reality and adds much more to the final product as a whole.

Nosferatu is a film that deserves to be seen by any fan of the genre as it truly was and still is one of the greatest horror gems in cinema history. Unfortunately, a lawsuit was launched against Marnau because his film so closely resembled *Dracula* and so his production company was ordered to destroy every copy that they had. Luckily, one copy survived and since then, has been duplicated many times and multiple versions are available online as well as on a restored version on Blu-Ray, which is absolutely magnificent.

Since *Nosferatu*, many more vampire films have been made and while some of them are good and some of them are not, the genre itself has taken off with velocity and universal appeal. Nearly everyone has heard of the classic Dracula tale and its influence within the horror genre has been unmistakably present and heard. Bela Lugosi would come to encapsulate the "classic Dracula" in 1931, with the widespread release of *Dracula* across North America. However, it is worth offering much deserved credence to Marnau's gothic masterpiece. Such an iconic figure really began with what is considered film's first cult movie: *Nosferatu*.

Highballing Through Gehenna

by John C. Foster

Groans and cries of protest erupted from the crowded station as a man in overalls climbed a ladder up to the giant board. The family watched as the man slid flat plaques onto the board.

The little girl: "What does it say, daddy?"

The father: "Sound it out, honey."

The little girl: "C-A...can...C-E...can-cell-ed?" She put too much emphasis on the E and D at the end of the word, but her father nodded absently.

The man in the overalls struggled to ignore the increasing number of shouts directed at him. Someone jostled his ladder and for a moment it looked like it might topple.

"The storms are comin' in, you fools!" The man in overalls shouted, angry and slightly frightened. He looked back at the board, tapping every departure where he had inserted a wooden plaque reading CANCELLED.

The noon departure he left unmolested. ON TIME it said. The father looked again at the three tickets he held, as if afraid they had changed while in his breast pocket.

Departure Time - 12:00.

~

"What the hell is that?" Oswego said, pointing a gnarled finger at a Pinkerton's belt.

"A grenade, captain," the Pinkerton said.

The locomotive chuffed, the sound of a plains lion claiming territory. A cloud of steam enveloped them where they stood on the platform while the passengers streamed past.

"They come with the storm, son," Oswego said. "Winds maybe sixty, seventy miles an hour. You throw that thing into the wind, where's it gonna go?"

Oswego pointed at the windows of a rapidly filling passenger car. "Maybe there? Maybe land on the tracks beneath a car, derail the whole train?"

"I'll get rid of it, sir," the Pinkerton said.

Oswego stepped closer, a towering man. The Pinkerton's eyes focused on the strong, white teeth in the dark, scarred face.

"Twenty three times I've made this run. We were hit four times, always in a storm, but never lost a train," Oswego said. "Be smart, son." He waved at a family walking past, a little girl with eyes wide enough to fall into. "This cargo is important."

~

Dalton Worth led his wife and daughter alongside the train, looking for car number five. The train was a massive thing, twenty cars long. Twenty cars with paint peeling from the sides, walls reinforced with two by fours and concertina wire. Twenty cars to carry them north away from the rising waters. Through storm country.

"Look daddy," Miri said. "That car is metal."

Dalton glanced at a car with sides of corrugated steel, wrapped in chain link fencing. He glanced at his wife, Celia, and she shook her head.

"Hey, it has two front cars," Miri said, pointing up ahead.

"Locomotives," Celia said anxiously. The sound and smell on the train platform were horribly present, the reality of their impending trip north no longer deniable. "One is just a backup."

But it wasn't. They had heard the stories. The great black steam engine belching clouds of smoke and sparks pulled the train, heaving with muscles of iron. The second locomotive had a different purpose, if the rumors were true.

"Ace-la," Miri said, sounding out the fading letters painted on the sleek siding. In a train built of cast-off parts, held together with duct tape and baling wire, the second locomotive was the strangest piece. It was shaped differently. And though older by far than the steam engine in front of it, the second locomotive hinted at a technology out of their reach.

"Acela," Dalton said. "I think it means *fast*."

"All aboard," the conductor said. A steam whistle shrieked and Miri covered her ears, laughing.

~

"Tickets please," the conductor said as he reached their row. Miri held up the three tickets and the conductor leaned forward with a serious expression on his face.

"This here says you're going all the way to Detroit, is that true?" He spoke up a bit to be heard over the rattle and clatter of the moving train.

"Yessir," Miri said. "My daddy said the capital is booming."

The conductor leaned back and laughed as he used his ticket puncher to mark their tickets. He slipped small red markers into the rail over their seats.

"That it is," the conductor said. "All you fine folks comin' up from the south have filled it 'til it's ready to bust. Sidewalks full of people day and night. Electric lights and all the food you want to eat. You like to eat?"

"Does she ever," Celia said, smiling.

"Any kind of food?" Miri asked.

"Any kind," the conductor said. "My favorite is fried chicken and waffles. You like fried chicken and waffles?"

Miri turned and buried her face in her mother's side, overcome by a sudden bout of what they called *the shy*.

"Thank you," Celia said to the conductor.

"That's alright, you folks gonna be alright," the conductor said. He turned to glance at Dalton, who was sitting across the aisle. "Just listen to the announcements when they come. You're in car five. Got that? Car five."

"Car five," Dalton said.

~

Dalton heard his name and jolted awake as Celia reached across the aisle and poked his shoulder.

"...recommend you close your blinds if you're on the west side of the train," the conductor was saying from the front of the car, his voice silencing the quiet conversation of the passengers. "I'll be back in about a half an hour, that's thirty minutes, folks, and give you the go ahead to open those blinds again."

He turned and slid open the door between cars, the volume and clatter increasing tremendously until he slid it closed behind him.

Celia leaned over and tugged their blinds down, glancing at Dalton.

"Oh Jesus," someone said a few rows behind them.

"Close them, close the blinds," another voice said.

A faint odor permeated the car. Smoke with something ugly and rotten underneath.

"It stinks," Miri said. Other voices were expressing similar sentiments.

"What is that?" A woman said.

Dalton mouthed a word to Celia, "Pittsburgh."

~

Oswego stood by the massive, spade shaped cowcatcher at the front of the locomotive and watched the engineers swing over the pipe from the wooden water tower beside the tracks to refill the train's tanks.

"Let's get that hooked up," he bellowed at a Pinkerton running a cable from the Acela locomotive to the telegraph tower. Six hours on the rails and the sun was beginning to set. Red light from the west limned the golden telegraph wires in fire.

Oswego walked forward, carefully stepping on the crossties, which always seemed to be just long of a normal stride. He was wearing his sidearm, a dull, gray .38 revolver with the still visible words *Smith & Wesson* stamped into the metal of the barrel. Every Pinkerton who stepped off the train carried a weapon, relic double barrel shotguns or single barrel scatterguns of newer make they called *Detroit Shooters*. Inside the train his men kept the weapons in lockers, at least during the day when most of the passengers were awake.

He glanced back and saw a few hardy souls sliding their windows down a bit, trying to get fresh air. He knew they could see the weapons his Pinkertons were carrying, but that was okay. Armed men outside the train made them feel safe. Armed men inside the train made them frightened, and he avoided triggering that primitive emotion if at all possible.

Far enough, he thought stepping off the tracks. He closed his eyes and lifted his face into the wind, sniffing deeply.

Ahh, dammit.

"Captain," his telegrapher said, running up the tracks.

"Where's your weapon?" Oswego said.

"Shit, sorry sir," the Pinkerton replied, torn between delivering his message and running back to the train to get his weapon.

"Report," Oswego said.

"Yessir. Weather report," the Pinkerton said. His cheeks were full and pink with rosacea. Oswego wondered how often he needed to shave.

"Out with it, son."

"Yessir," the Pinkerton said. "Storms coming in fast. We're not gonna make it through in time."

Oswego smiled, letting his teeth show. "That's alright, I was just thinking our girl here needs a bath." The trains were always female, just the way it was. "And the Deformation?"

The Pinkerton swallowed. Oswego thought this might be the kid's virgin run. "Significant Deformation, sir."

Oswego nodded.

"They gave us clearance to highball it, sir," the Pinkerton said.

Oswego nodded. "Go on back and confirm to base we are adjusting to condition orange, then pass the word."

"Orange, yessir."

Oswego looked out over the flat land, marked here and there by jagged tree stumps and the empty frames of houses. The terrain had a scoured look. New maps issued a few years back designated this stretch of nothing as The Barrens, but the term didn't take and folks still called it by a name given to it by the briefly resurgent Old Testament movement.

Gehenna. The place of punishment.

Captain Oswego's hand rested on the butt of his revolver as he lifted his nose into the wind again.

Hell on the wind and that was a fact.

~

"Look, daddy," Miri said as she followed Dalton back from the café car. He glanced where she pointed, trying to maintain balance and not dump the cardboard tray of sandwiches and drinks he was carrying.

Pinkertons were moving around the train now, casually pacing between the rows of seats. There was a great deal of tightening of belts and tugging on hat brims, pulling them low over the eyes. Some wore pistols of various makes but more carried shotguns. One woman, an officer of some sort, carried a small, stubby weapon somewhere in between a pistol and a rifle. Tightly machined pieces of black metal and plastic that screamed of old tech.

"Sorry," Miri said, stumbling into a seated woman who reached out and steadied the little girl.

"'S'alright, sugar," the woman said. Her eyes met Dalton's for a moment and she glanced at one of the Pinkertons.

"C'mon, honey," Dalton said.

Back in their own car he paused as the conductor stepped aside to let them pass.

"I notice we've picked up speed, sir," Dalton said.

"Nothing to worry about," the conductor said. He leaned over to Miri. "They gave us the go ahead to *highball*. Now ain't that a funny word?"

Miri smiled. "What's highball?"

"Means go fast," the conductor said. "Now go on and take your seats 'fore those sandwiches turn to cardboard."

"They didn't have any chicken and waffles," Miri blurted out as they passed.

The conductor turned and Dalton saw the effort it took to compose his face into a smile. "Too messy for a train, each person needs twenty napkins to eat."

"Twenty napkins!" Miri said.

The conductor nodded seriously. "You'll get all you want in Detroit."

~

A horrendous screech from the overhead speakers woke Dalton from slumber and he jerked upright in his seat. The car erupted in startled questions until the screech abruptly cut off.

"It's alright, baby," Celia said, holding Miri. Dalton looked over, able to see his daughter's too-wide eyes in the dim lighting coming from the oil lamps swinging on hooks at either end of the car.

Static filled the air and another screech caused Miri to slap her hands over her ears. "What is it, mommy?"

"—tion, please. Attention please, cars one through seven. All women and children proceed immediately to the security car, car number eight. Proceed immediately to the security car, car number eight." The loudspeaker popped and crackled like grease on a hot skillet.

Dalton heard a loud roar and the train shuddered on the tracks. "What the hell was that?"

"Attention please, cars nine through eighteen, please proceed to the aft security car, car number nineteen. Repeat, if you are a woman or child in cars nine through eighteen, proceed immediately to the security car in the rear, car number nineteen."

Everywhere people were rising, confused, as the conductor began to push through the crowd. "Men, stay in your seats, let the women and children through. Okay people, let's move it, nice and orderly back to car number eight."

"What's happening?" A man screeched, reaching for the conductor's arm.

"Sit in your seat, sir. Women and children, let's move." The conductor doused the oil lantern closest to him and shadows engulfed the car, eliciting fearful cries.

"Celia, go, go," Dalton said.

"Daddy?" Miri cried.

"Go with mommy," Dalton said, his eyes on his wife's drawn face. "Go hon, go."

"Oh God," Celia said, but she was already moving, dragging Miri by the arm into the aisle and the tide of people surging towards the rear.

The car shuddered again and Dalton watched Celia steady their daughter.

Popping and crackling from the loudspeaker drowned out the people in the car. "Gentlemen, remain seated until the aisles are clear. Repeat, remain seated until the aisles are clear."

~

Celia and Miri pressed into the milling crowd in the security car, shoved forward by people entering behind them. The car had no seats and she grabbed an overhead strap for balance, her free hand locked into Miri's shoulder.

"Stay right next to me," Celia said.

"Where's daddy?"

"He's alright, he's watching—"

"Attention, attention," the loudspeakers blared. "All able bodied men between the ages of 16 and 60 will report to the armories. All able bodied men will report to the armories."

"Oh no…" Celia said, her voice weak. The crowd pressed in and she found it hard to breath.

"Let me out," a woman screamed, pounding at the door. "Henry! Henry!"

"Mommy," Miri said, pressing her face into her mother's belly. Celia could feel the wetness of tears through her blouse.

"We'll be alright, baby."

Glass bulbs in mesh cages overhead flared into brilliance and Celia felt a new vibration through her feet as the dry smell of ozone filled the air.

~

Oswego gathered five Pinkertons in the Acela engine car, all armed with old tech shotguns and sidearms. The kid with rosacea was among them, nervously spinning the barrel on a matte black .38, comforted by the winking presence of shells in the chambers.

"Warmin' it up," the chief engineer said, flipping switches in the cockpit. Lights began to shine and the nature of the vibration under their feet changed.

"How much range do we have?" Oswego said.

"Enough diesel for 25 miles at full speed," the engineer said, tapping a fuel gauge.

"Right then," Oswego said. "Please wait for my go ahead."

Debris was hitting the train at a furious rate, a thousand percussionists beating the outside of the car. A large chunk slammed into the carriage and Oswego thought *bass drum*.

"We hold this car, gentlemen," Oswego said. He patted the rosacea kid on the shoulder. "Put that away before you shoot someone in the ass, huh?"

A couple other Pinkertons laughed and the tension dropped a level. The kid holstered his pistol, blushing furiously.

"Name?" Oswego said.

"Porfoy, sir," the kid said, touching fingers to the brim of his hat.

"We're gonna hold this here Acela car, Porfoy, or the whole train dies. You hear?"

"Yessir," Porfoy said. "Loud and clear."

A giant thump rocked through the train, radiating back from the front. The engineer picked up a radio headset and listened, then nodded at Oswego. A soldier peered through the window into the roiling storm and jerked back.

"Here they come!"

~

It was fast, chaotic, impossible to understand and most of all absurd.

"You and you, refuse to the east," the Pinkerton had said as he jammed blunt, single barreled shotguns in their hands along with sacks full of charges and buckshot rounds. "You and you, refuse to the west."

"Refuse what?" Dalton said, but was ignored.

"This is insane," Shore said, pushing his thick glasses up on his nose. He closed the breach on the second of their two Detroit Shooters. "You see anything?"

Dalton shook his head and sneezed at the grit filling the air. The train shook and his forehead bounced off the window. "Dammit," he said. "Just flying sand. The sky is green."

"You guys ready?" The old guy called from further up the car, peering out to the east while his loader double checked their two shooters.

"No!" Dalton called back, earning a glare from the old man. When the

Pinkerton in the armory had said he was too old, the gray hair had bared his forearm.

"What was that tattoo?" Dalton called, trying to focus his careening thoughts on something. Anything.

"USMC," the grizzled man said, baring the arm again and waving it at Dalton and Shore as if that meant something.

A string of pops echoed back to them. The train juddered sideways and righted itself.

"What was that?" Shore said.

"Gunfire," the old man shouted back. "Get ready."

Dalton picked up one of the guns and dropped to a knee so he wouldn't trip and shoot himself. Things grew distant, his sensory input coming from far away even as his bowels turned to water.

"I don't wanna do this," Shore said. "You ever fire a gun?"

"I'm an English teacher," Dalton said.

Pop-pop-pop.

"They're into the next car," the old man called out over the roar of the train.

~

Celia hugged Miri close to her, fighting to stay on her feet as the mass of people shifted. The security car was jerking and shaking constantly, the noise deafening. Children and adults alike were openly sobbing in fear.

A massive thump shook the car and it rolled sideways until the entire crowd was pressed against the right hand wall. In the same moment, the lights overhead dimmed and there was a tremendous crack and flash of light visible through the safety shutters. A deafening scream drowned out all other noise before the security car righted itself. The stink of burned meat filled the car.

"What was that?"

"Help me, I broke my arm!"

"Mommy, what's happening?" Miri cried up at her mother.

"The train is protecting us," Celia said, rubbing her daughter's hair.

The lights dimmed once more and again came the terrible crack as blue light flooded the car. They choked on the burning smell.

~

It happened too fast. One second Dalton was crouched, listening to the battle raging elsewhere on the train. In the next second a section of the roof was peeled open and a cyclone of sand immediately filled their car.

A Detroit Shooter boomed and Dalton saw the flash even as something came pouring down through the hole. It tumbled inside like a fall of giant maggots and

Dalton leveled his gun, afraid to fire because of the other men.

"Shoot!" Shore yelled into his ear and Dalton heard screams from the maelstrom at the front of the car.

He braced the weapon and fired, the butt crashing painfully into the meat of his shoulder. "Reload!"

He handed the weapon blindly off to Shore and took the loaded Shooter in exchange. His finger went slack on the trigger and his jaw dropped as *something* surged towards him.

"Oh God!" Shore cried.

~

Oswego pressed his eyes to the periscope and angled the viewer back down along the length of the train. A huge, seething pile of the Deformation had swarmed over several cars. More of the Deformation rode in on the winds, giant kites made of flesh with dozens of grasping hands and screaming mouths. A brief flash of memory, pizza makers at Luigi's tossing circles of spinning dough high into the air. His stomach lurched.

Crack! A bright flash lit up the storm and Oswego saw a cloud of flame roll back along the length of the train.

"We are a rocket on rails, boys," Oswego said.

Gunfire crashed from the train, his men shooting through specially designed firing slits. Porfoy released the cylinder on his .38, dumping brass shells onto the floor and fumbling in fresh rounds. He was repeating something over and over but Oswego couldn't make it out.

More flashes from the security cars as the electrified defenses cooked the attacking Deformation into cinders.

"That's it, we're not gonna hold," Oswego said, looking away from the periscope and tapping the white faced engineer on the shoulder. "Crank her up, full speed!"

~

It was people. A stretching mass of screaming, howling people all connected, arms grafted into bellies, feet into heads, hips into backs. They were dangling, stretching through the hole in the ceiling like pulsating dough and Dalton wondered in horror at how much of it was still outside the train.

He aimed at the mass and pulled the trigger. A gout of blood exploded as the buckshot struck the squirming flesh. "Reload!" He said, turning when Shore didn't take the weapon.

The other man was lying on his back between two seats, unconscious.

"Shore!" Dalton dropped to his knees, patting around for the sack of ammunition, unable to take his eyes off the horror stretching towards him.

Small hands grabbed the top of the seat as an individual form no larger than a child struggled to pull itself free, skin tearing with a grotesque, adhesive sound.

Bile filled Dalton's throat when he saw that other heads on the mass were twisting, teeth chewing to free the child-thing until it was dangling from an elongating piece of indeterminate meat stretching from its forehead.

The train gave a mighty lurch beneath him and Dalton rolled backwards, banging his shoulders into the ground, driving the wind from his lungs.

~

The flashing blue light and crackling thunder had grown into a constant assault on their senses inside the security car. Smoke roiled along the ceiling and the stench of vomit competed with the grotesquely appealing stink of roasting pork.

Celia lost her grip on Miri when the train lunged forward, pitching everyone towards the rear of the car.

"Miri!"

Screams of pain and terror filled the car as it rattled and shook. The lights overhead dimmed and even amidst the chaos, Celia could feel an incredible surge of speed.

"Mommy!"

Was that Miri? "I'm here, baby! Miri, I'm here!"

~

"Seventy six miles per hour," the engineer said, grinning with fierce pride. "Full speed."

Oswego could feel the velocity through his boots, the train seeming to ride higher and lighter on the rails. The rattle of gunfire tapered off as the Pinkertons leaned back, white eyes staring from faces coated with black grime, coughing against the stink of cordite. Bright shell casings bounced like popcorn kernels on the vibrating floor.

"Well done," Oswego said to the engineer, carefully stepping back to the periscope. Through the brutal storm he saw no mass of attacking Deformation. No flames or flashes of lethal electricity. He rotated the periscope, stepping in a small circle inside the Acela car until he was looking forward along the train.

Porfoy saw his captain's white teeth as the big man grinned.

"What is it, sir?" Porfoy said.

"Clear sky ahead, gentlemen," Oswego said, smiling wider as the Pinkertons gave an exhausted cheer. "Give me ten more minutes at this speed and then lets throttle back."

Porfoy looked dazed. He had fired over thirty six rounds and his hand was cramping. "We did it," he said.

~

Dazed, Dalton sat up on the floor between two seats as the train began to decelerate. The hole in the ceiling channeled great currents of wind through the car, clearing it of smoke. Dalton rubbed grit from his eyes.

The thing that had tried to come in through the ceiling was gone.

Dalton heard a faint sound. An odd sound. And it took him nearly a minute to realize what it was. People were cheering in other cars on the train.

He grinned stupidly and reached over to pat Shore on the leg. "Hey, hey, it's over."

Shore groaned and touched his face. "I need my glasses."

"What happened to you?" Dalton asked, levering himself up until he could grab the seat back in front of him.

"I don't know," Shore said. "I think I…"

Shore's words faded into a dull, roaring sound as Dalton stood and saw the naked thing lurching blindly in the aisle.

It was no bigger than a child but obviously male and covered with odd, torn wounds, the worst of which covered the portion of its face from its hairline to the bridge of its nose. The white of its skull was visible through the missing skin and it flailed about uttering odd, feral sounds. Its eye sockets were empty, black holes lined in red.

"What is it?" Shore said, but Dalton ignored him, picking up a fallen scattergun. He aimed it and pulled the trigger. The hammer fell with a dry click.

"Worth, what is it?" Shore said again as Dalton walked carefully up the aisle so as not to stumble from the rocking of the train.

The thing heard him and turned, hands reaching, fingers grasping.

Dalton took the Detroit Shooter by the barrel, adjusting both hands to find his grip, then swung it on an angle. The sounds emerging from the thing changed, becoming higher pitched as he kept on swinging the weapon. He imagined he was chopping wood and settled into a rhythm until the Shooter's stock shattered and the thing lay unmoving and nearly shapeless from the blows. His face was lined with streaks of red by then, his hands and arms coated with blood and whitish bits of bone up to the elbows. When Shore finally located his glasses and saw Dalton, he fainted for the second time that evening.

~

Celia limped alongside the tracks, holding Miri by the hand. A crowd of women and children and a few old men moved with them, some in shock, some exclaiming at the state of the train.

The security car was a scorched mess with blackened chunks of organic material fused into the siding. The rest of the train cars, every single one, were dripping. Great rivers of red and flowing gobbets of meat drizzled and plopped onto the tracks.

"Look over there, honey, are those mountains?" Celia said, trying in vain to distract her daughter.

"It smells really bad," Miri said.

"I know, hon."

Windows had been punched in and great sections of roofing on several peeled up as if by a giant's can-opener. Crews were hurriedly nailing boards and stretching tarps over the injuries sustained by the train.

"Ten minutes, people," the big captain said, striding past them. "We mount up in ten minutes, please return to your original seating assignments."

They found Dalton sitting beside the tracks, staring vacantly into the distance.

"Are you hurt? Dalton, are you hurt?"

Celia rushed to him, taking his red stained hands in hers and looking everywhere for injuries.

"Your daddy here's a hero," the conductor said, walking over to them and patting Miri on the top of her head. "Held onto car number five almost by himself."

Dalton pulled Miri into his arms and Celia knelt, embracing them both. Still, he couldn't resist looking over his daughter's shoulder at the conductor.

"Hey," Dalton said.

"Yeah?" The conductor said, adjusting a bandage on his forearm.

"What if that ever comes…ever gets up to…"

The conductor shook his head and smiled. "Ain't never gonna happen. Waters rising in the south, and the storms are making the middle something awful, but up north, in Detroit City? We got the electricity going and people filling the sidewalks day and night."

"And all you can eat?" Miri said, glancing up with big eyes.

The conductor laughed. "You got it, honey. All you can eat, any time you want it."

~

Oswego stood at the front of the black locomotive, watching as crewmen used long hooks to tug free the mountain of gore stacked up against the cowcatcher.

"Porfoy," he said, and the young Pinkerton ran up. "Hook into the telegraph and report contact with the Deformation. Inform them of the location." He knelt and spread out a map on the crossties, using his Smith & Wesson to hold down one corner. "See here? That was the point of contact."

Porfoy knelt and studied the map, noting that the captain's finger was touching a place outside of the red zone denoting The Barrens.

"But sir, that's at least twenty miles north of the general contact zone," Porfoy said. He looked at past contact points marked on the map and drew a chilling conclusion. "That's twenty miles closer to Detroit than any other recorded contact."

Oswego glanced back at the bloody train and watched the people boarding. "I know, son. I know."

John C. Foster was born in Sleepy Hollow, NY, and has been afraid of the dark for as long as he can remember. A writer of horror stories and thrillers, Foster spent many years in the ersatz glow of Los Angeles before relocating to the relative sanity of New York City where he lives with his lady, Linda, and their intrepid dog, Coraline. Foster's stories can be found in *Dark Visions Vol. 2* (**Grey Matter Press**), *Under the Stairs* (**Wicked East Press**) and *Big Book of New Short Horror* (**Pill Hill Press**) among other fine collections. He has recently completed his first novel, *Dead Men*, and is hard at work on his second novel, *The Isle*.

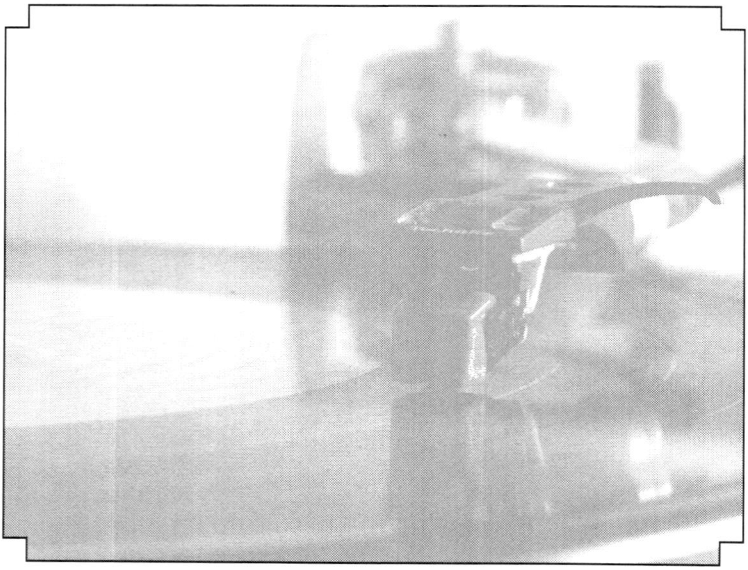

We Share the Dark

by Carlie St. George

When the ghost sat beside me, I was sitting on the porch, considering suicide the same idle way people think about where they'd go on vacation if they could afford to. Pills and knives were popular but also prone to failure. Hanging was so old-fashioned as to be almost charming, but if your neck don't break, it would be one lousy way to go. A shotgun was practical. Already had one, and I didn't think I could fuck it up any. I was warming to the idea when the ghost put its hands around my wrist and squeezed till I dropped my cigarette.

"Fine," I said. "Cancer's not an option anyway. Takes too damn long."

~

The ghost rarely let himself be seen, and he never spoke out loud at all. But I knew his name was Alex because ghosts are better than anyone at nonverbal communication.

He spoke through gestures, through charades, through temper tantrums. Used to be a theater student, somewhere out west, and clearly he missed putting on a show. I would wake, sometimes, to the clashing of pots and pans, bad renditions of Led Zeppelin and Black Sabbath songs. Alex usually started up before even God was awake, but I'd put up with worse before, and I knew I'd put up with more after.

Only sometimes did he touch me. His fingers pushed against my skin, inside it, and I would know things about him, the little things that made up a person. He knew things about me too, only the bits I was willing to give. We didn't share our secrets or our fears or our childhoods, only pieces folk don't usually bother putting into words.

~

A few weeks after Alex arrived, my ex-boyfriend came over to see if I had one of his old Muddy Waters albums. Rob only listened to vinyl—his Daddy hated technology something fierce, and he had once broken a CD by throwing it across the room, slashing the hell out of Rob's left ear on the way. That was some twenty years gone now, but scars remember, and Rob had a lot of scars.

Alex and I were watching some dumb comedy on TV—or I was watching, while Alex objected by launching teddy bears round the room. Rob walked in without knocking and eyed the floating bears cautiously as he leaned back against the wall.

"So," he said. "Nothing's changed, I guess."

One of the teddy bears—the blue one my daddy had bought me, two weeks before he left town for good—wiggled its blue butt right in front of Rob's face. Rob slapped it with the back of his hand, the way you'd slap a woman.

I watched him watch his hands, curl them into fists and shove them in his pockets. "This one love you too?" Rob asked, staring at the ground

Beside me, Alex flickered.

"Doubt it," I said. "Hasn't even peeked at me in the shower yet. Frankly, I'm offended."

"Right," Rob said. "Well."

I sighed. Rob's almost total lack of humor had always been his worst selling point. "I'll look again, but I don't think it's here. You only brought that turntable over a couple of times."

"Can't think of where else it'd be."

I couldn't either—Rob didn't have much of a social life—so I left him by the door to have a look around. Alex hovered over my shoulder, let his fingers melt right through my skin. I saw purple bruises, wide eyes. Commercials for Lifetime movies.

"No," I told him. "It wasn't like that at all."

I couldn't find the record. I came back into the living room, found Rob staring through the screen door at the setting sun, arms folded loosely across his chest. I missed those arms, those shoulders. The dead might touch me, but they were always cold.

"Sorry," I told him. "Nothing doing. Might be you could find another copy down at the Salvation Army."

Rob shook his head. "You know he'll leave you. They always do."

I pushed past him and kicked open the door.

"Well," I said. "The living are pretty good at that, too."

~

Alex wasn't a blues man like Rob. He didn't like country music either, took the Bible from my bedside and underlined Luke 6:36—*Be merciful, just as your Father is merciful*—when I started playing Hank Aaron one morning. He didn't even like Patsy Cline.

I didn't ask him what music he did like. I didn't ask him where he was from, what his last name was, how he died. Figured he'd tell me when he wanted to talk.

Course, he didn't want to talk. He wanted me to guess. Alex liked playing games, and I didn't, but I *did* like the way that he laughed, loud, like it had never occurred to him that the dead ought to be quiet. So I indulged him by playing Twenty Questions, and he kept score by drawing lipstick tallies on the wall. I didn't have a lot of lipstick. When I ran out, I drove my truck down to Wal-Mart and bought a Ouija board from the bargain bin. Alex loved it, could spend hours spelling out nothing more than knock-knock and yo momma jokes. He said he was a big kid at heart. Said he was only nineteen.

I called bullshit on that pretty fast.

D-O-N-T Y-O-U B-E-L-

I forced the planchette to NO.

W-H-Y N-O-T

"'Cause you're a liar, Alex."

His hands slipped away from mine, and I shook my head. "Don't take offense," I said. "I don't think you mean nothing by it. Comes second nature to you, I expect, but you're still a bullshitter, through and through, and I can't trust anything you tell me if it don't come straight out of your skin."

For a moment, I sensed nothing, and I thought Alex had left me to sulk, the way some men do when a woman has the gall to be honest. I didn't much care—I wasn't about to apologize for speaking my mind in my own house, and anyway, it was too hot to get all worked up. The air was damp and suffocating, and every inch of me was beaded with sweat.

I leaned back against the couch and took a long drink of my beer, and Alex's fingers wrapped around my wrist, gently squeezing until I set the bottle down. "It's like you don't want me to do anything fun," I complained. "Can't smoke. Can't drink. Can't listen to country."

He didn't respond to that, just guided my hands back to the planchette, his fingers becoming visible between mine. They were long and dark and refreshingly cold. His fingernails were too clean for this part of the country.

"You don't usually let me see," I murmured.

B-U-R-N S-C-A-R-S D-E-F-O-R-M-E-D H-I-D-E-O-U-S

I smiled. "Liar," I said softly.

Alex moved the planchette to YES. After a moment's hesitation, his fingers disappeared. The Bible, which had been pushed off the coffee table to make room for my Burger King wrappers and beer, lifted in the air. Pages flipped back and forth until Alex found what he was looking for and set the Good Book in my lap.

It took me a minute to scan the page and read the line he wanted read. "So we fix our eyes not on what is seen, but on what is unseen. For what is seen is temporary, but what is unseen is eternal." I looked up at where I thought he might be sitting. "So...you're saying you're not just a pretty face?"

Alex didn't laugh like I thought he would. He grabbed at my wrists again, and this time I felt his cold fingers sink inside mine and hold there. I saw the boy he once was, a chubby thing with big eyes and bigger hair, playing in a costume box, performing for an audience of stuffed animals and two hamsters. He always played cops, never robbers. He recited movie lines to himself on the way to school. If he could dress the part, he could play the part, and maybe someday people would believe he *was* the part—

I pulled back, blowing warm air into my hands. My fingers had gone so cold they'd started to ache.

"You don't gotta be no one special for me," I told him. "I like you. You should like you too."

He kissed me, and I tasted birthday cake, strawberries, and vanilla frosting. I smelled smoke and counted candles, twenty-seven of them, waiting to be blown out.

I wasn't so much older, and Alex kissed like he'd been born for it, but his tongue was as cold as his hands, and it was only a matter of time before he left like they all left. "You're a little dead for me," I said, stepping away and hugging my arms around my waist. "Might be best to keep things platonic."

For a moment, there was nothing. Then the planchette moved across the Ouija board. K-N-O-C-K K-N-O-C-K.

"Who's there?"

Y-O M-O-M-M-A.

I shook my head. "I need to teach you some actual jokes."

~

Rob came by again while I was at the grocery store. I pulled a bag full of peanut butter and booze out of my truck and found him sitting on the porch, staring at his boots like there were stories written on them.

"You missing another record?" I asked him.

He didn't look up. "Grandfather's watch."

I didn't even remember the watch. "Are you sure Boxer isn't eating your stuff?"

"Doubt it. Died a month ago."

"Sorry," I said, and meant it. Boxer was dumb as a bag of bricks, but he was a good dog. Had been.

"Yeah." Rob looked up. There were circles under his eyes, and circles under the circles. "Need help with that?"

I considered my pride, shrugged it away, and handed him the grocery bag so I could fish my keys out of my purse. When I opened the door, I took the bag back. "Come on in," I said.

The house was a mess. I wasn't worried—Rob's house was always a mess too, although his walls probably had less lipstick on them. I watched him look around as I poured myself a shot of bourbon. "Same ghost?" he asked finally, turning back at me.

"Same one," I said. Alex was being quiet, but he was somewhere nearby—the house felt different, heavier, when the dead were in the room. "He hasn't heard the bells yet."

"There was that one girl, the girl in the closet—"

"Adele."

Rob nodded. "She was here—what?—seven months before she heard them?"

"Six," I said. Alex had been here almost three. Sometimes they were only here for days, even hours, before they were gone again. "You can look 'round for the watch, if you want, but I don't think it's here."

Rob looked. He couldn't find it. I offered him a shot, to be polite, and he took one but didn't drink it. He turned the glass round and round in his hands. I glanced out the window and noticed that my truck was the only one in front of the house.

"I walked," he said before I could ask. "Needed the air."

It was almost six miles from my house to his. I looked at his face again and was surprised I didn't see it sooner. "I thought this new home was working out for him."

Rob scrubbed his hands over his face. "It was," he said. "But you know how he is."

He was a violent, mean sonofabitch. "Yeah."

"I was a fool to think it'd last." Rob finally took his shot, automatically went to pour himself another, stopped, and looked at me. I nodded, but his fingers hesitated around the bottle just the same. He drew his hand back. "Anyway, I should get on home."

I followed him out to the porch. "I could give you a ride."

Rob shook his head. "Not in any hurry. A nurse comes a few days a week now, checks up on him when I have to run out. They aren't expecting me for a few hours." He started down the driveway, stopped, and turned back to look at me. "Look. I'm sorry for how things turned out between us."

I had never heard Rob apologize for anything, not in twenty-five years. I didn't know what to say.

"It's okay you're still mad. I said some shitty things. You didn't deserve most of them. But I'm worried about you."

I laughed. "Me? Rob, you look like you ain't slept in a week."

Rob shrugged. "I'm fine," he said. "It's been busy on the farm, is all."

"Rob—"

"No one's seen you anywhere. Not at the bowling alley, not at the bar, not even for the fireworks last week. Judi says you been calling out sick—"

I stared at him incredulously. "You been spying on me?"

"I ran into her at the gas station," Rob said calmly. "She was worried. Says it's like you barely leave the house."

"I just went to the grocery store!"

"Yeah, and how long's it been since the last trip?" He stepped closer to me. "You're skin and bones, Etta. You can't keep doing this to yourself. It's not healthy, spending all your time with the dead."

I laughed. "You're going to talk to me about what's healthy? You?"

"Etta—"

"No, just—just get the hell out of here. Go home."

Rob nodded. He turned and started down the road, but only a few seconds later, he stopped and turned around. "You think I was jealous," he said. "And maybe I was sometimes, but that's not why it ended like it did. I know those ghosts mean a lot to you. I know you love them, but Etta, you need to be more careful, you're going to end up one of them, and I don't want to watch that."

"Then don't look," I said, and headed back inside.

~

I headed straight for Jim Beam, and Alex's fingers found my wrist again. "The hell do you care?" I asked, spitefully tugging out of his grip and pouring myself the shot.

He touched my face gently.

"Asshole." But I let go of the glass.

I walked into the living room and fell back on the couch, kicking off my shoes with more vehemence than they deserved. "This is why you don't screw your best friend. You lose one, you lose both, and then who do you talk to?"

Alex touched my face again. Cold radiated down the side of my neck.

"You don't talk," I reminded him. "Won't. You just play your little charades. And besides that, you're dead, and that means I lose you too."

His hands were on both sides of my face now, sinking straight on through. I closed my eyes and saw church bells and question marks.

"Don't know if they're church bells," I told him. "I don't even know what they are. God? Another medium? I can't hear em. Only the dead. And it's always the same—ghost finds me, stays a while, hears the bells, has to follow em. Once he's gone, he don't come back. New ghost comes instead. Rinse, repeat."

Alex kissed me then, and there wasn't nothing platonic about it. I let him because I was lonely, because I missed someone touching me, even if his touch made me shiver for all the wrong reasons. But I told him he couldn't save me, that no one beat the bells, and I sure couldn't afford to believe otherwise. It hurt too much, believing, and it was so damn easy to do.

But folk, living or dead, well, they hear what they want, don't they, and Alex didn't want to listen. He lowered himself on top of me and into me and into me, and we became one person, at least for a little while. I knew how cookies smelled, fresh out of his momma's oven; and I knew how blood tasted, as it came up through his throat. I knew if he *had* committed suicide, he'd have done it by jumping off the Golden Gate Bridge.

I kept my eyes closed during. Didn't want to see that I couldn't see him.

Afterwards, I was shaking too much to sleep. I huddled underneath every blanket I owned, and I heard whispers in the dark, more like echoes than actual words. *Ever...ever...ever...oh...oh...oh.*

Never go, he was saying. I'll never let go.

~

We had two months together.

Alex performed Shakespearean tragedies with my teddy bears. Made sounds instead of words, so it was like listening to an adult in one of them Peanuts cartoons, only a lot more melodramatic. Took me forever to figure out what he was doing, and sometimes he still had to cheat, touch my skin and fill it with soliloquys. I liked it, when he cheated.

We watched black-and-white comedies. I put on Willie Nelson just to see him bitch. We spent whole days lying together, swapping stories without saying a word.

And then we were sitting on the couch, watching *The Apartment*, and I heard him breathe in sharply.

And I knew.

~

Alex tried to fight it, of course, spent days trying to shake it off. Kept asking me to turn up the volume. Kept laughing too hard, too much. He tried to tell me what it felt like, showed me a white rabbit and a pocket watch. *I'm late; I'm late for a very important date.* But he couldn't remember what the date was for.

By the end, he could barely hear me. The bells got louder the longer they were ignored, and Alex kept asking me what I had said, sometimes even forgetting what he was saying. He tried to distract me, make me laugh. He performed *Romeo and Juliet* because it was my favorite to mock. But he kept losing focus, and the teddy bears kept crashing to the floor.

When we went to bed that night, he showed me sunlight and kisses and bacon. He was telling me he'd see me in the morning.

Alex was a liar. But this time, I let it slide.

~

When Rob walked up the driveway, I was sitting on the porch, drinking a beer and idly thinking how I wouldn't be leaving anybody. Everyone I could leave had already left. I'd blow out the back of my skull and maybe chase the bells myself for a change. It was a comforting notion.

"Look, I really don't got any of your things," I told him.

He sat down beside me. "I know."

"You ever find the record?"

"Never went missing."

I stared at him.

"Sorry," he said.

Two apologies in one year. I'd be worried if I wasn't so pissed. "Your granddaddy didn't even have a watch, did he?"

Rob shrugged. "He might've. Never passed it on, though."

"So, you been coming over...why? See if I was miserable and lost without you?"

"Didn't have nothing to do with us. I just wanted to see you were okay. And you weren't, but then I didn't know what to do about it." He scratched the side of his face where a beard was starting to grow in. "Guess I made a mess of things."

"You guess." I shook my head. "So, when I said you were spying on me a couple months ago..."

"I really did run into Judi; but yeah, I was spying."

"*Why?*"

Rob didn't answer right away. He pulled a pack of cigarettes out of his pocket and casually swiped my lighter, like we were ten again. "That day we fought, I'd come by to take you to the movies. You remember?"

I did. Going to the movies was a special occasion—the theater was over an hour away.

"Figured you'd be on the porch, but you weren't. So I came inside and called your name. Called it three times, but you didn't answer."

"I fell asleep," I said.

Rob ignored me. "You had to be in the bedroom. You weren't anywhere else, but the door was shut, and I didn't want to open it. I was scared to."

"Of *what*? Finding me on my knees, blowing a ghost?"

He threw his cigarette to the ground. "God's hooks, Etta. I was scared of finding you dead."

"Dead—"

Rob shook his head. After a minute, he stomped out the cigarette and methodically lit another one. "Your ghost is gone," he said.

I couldn't see how Alex had anything to do with anything, but I didn't rush him. Rob got to places in his own time. "Yeah," I said. "Well, that's what they do. Remember?"

He ignored that too. "I could always tell," Rob said. "I can't see 'em, can't hear 'em, but it's different when they're gone. You're different. It's like you...fade just a little.

"When I said what I said, about you loving them more than me, I didn't mean you were *in* love with them. I meant—that little girl, Adele—you took to her like she was your own, and when she was gone, and that door was closed, and I kept calling your name, and with that shotgun you keep by your bed—"

"Okay," I said.

Rob stopped.

"You want a beer?" I asked.

He nodded.

I went inside and got two more beers. When I came back out, Rob was looking down at his hands again. His fingernails were dirty. So were mine.

"I wouldn't have done it," I said. "Everyone thinks about it sometimes, but I'd never really do it, you know."

"It's just...you could be happy, I think. You don't have to invite them in. I know you can't stop them from coming, but you don't have to talk to em, take care of em. Hell, if you left this podunk town and actually went somewhere, maybe you could even outrun em. Find someone living to love."

"I have someone here."

"Yeah?"

"He's kind of an asshole."

Rob smiled. "Yeah. He is."

"He taught me how to ride a horse, and I taught him how to smoke a cigarette."

"You also got him through high school."

"You'd have gotten there."

He snorted. "Not likely."

"Hey." Rob didn't look at me, so I took him by the hands. His skin was sweaty and solid, and it told me nothing at all. I could never know Rob the way I knew Alex, could never touch his skin and see the things he didn't have voice for, but I still knew him better than anyone else alive.

"Your daddy," I said, "is a mean sonofabitch, and I wish you'd stop listening to the lies he's been selling. There's more to brains than numbers, Rob, and there's more to a man than how hard he hits."

"It wasn't so bad," Rob said. "Lots of folk round here, *they* have it bad. It wasn't—"

I squeezed his wrist gently, and Rob stopped.

"It was bad," I told him. "It was, and you don't owe that man a damn thing. The way he treated you, your momma, you should have let him rot outside whatever nursing home kicked him out. You shouldn't be bathing him, changing him, listening to him rant and rave...but that's what you're gonna do, isn't it?"

Rob shrugged. Didn't say anything for a while. Finally, "He's my blood, Etta."

"Shouldn't make him your responsibility." I drank from my beer and set it aside, scooted closer to him on the porch. "You want I should go on some road trip, find a new life, leave the ghosts behind? Tell you what: I will if you will. How about it?"

Rob looked at me.

~

"Wallet?"

"Got it."

"Suitcase?"

"In the back. You know, maybe we should just skip your place. Don't stop there at all."

"Can't. No spare clothes, and I don't think I'll fit in your jeans. Booze?"

"In the suitcase."

"Lighter?"

"In my purse. Shit, did you grab the peanut butter?"

Rob sounded offended. "Of course."

"Good." I put on my seatbelt. "Good. That's good."

The keys were in my hand.

I looked at them, and then past them, up through the windshield at my little blue house. House where I learned to read, where my momma died, where I met my very first ghost, playing hide and seek in a kitchen cupboard, but I wasn't the only one hiding there. Little blue house where I knew the walls like I knew my very own skin. No surprises there, no dangers. I understood everything it expected of me.

I looked at the little house and then the open road and the horizon just stretching on and on.

The keys were in my hand. But I just couldn't breathe.

Rob swallowed. "It's okay, Etta."

"It's not."

"I know."

"I want to."

"I know."

"It's just..."

"I *know*."

I turned to look at him. "I can't," I said. "I can't." He didn't say anything. "You don't look mad."

Rob shrugged, leaned back, didn't say nothing for a while. "Maybe I am," he said finally. "Maybe a little. I don't know. Reckon we were never going to get very far. Wake up in the morning, probably drive right on back. No one makes it out, Etta. No one leaves it all behind."

"No one hears the bells," I said. "Only the dead."

We sat there for a while. Eventually, Rob unbuckled his seatbelt and kissed me on the cheek. "Come on. I'll fix you dinner."

I nodded. Dropped the keys.

~

Rob made me Pop-Tarts for dinner because I didn't have shit in my fridge. He went on about that for a while. I mostly ignored him. Then we sat on the porch till the stars came out, drinking beer and talking about parts of the world we'd like to see someday. Wasn't so different from thinking how you'd kill yourself, if you could afford to.

Rob had his daddy, and I had my ghosts, and we both knew we'd keep doing what we were doing till we were dead. But it was good to have someone to share it with again, the dark things that kept you from chasing bells, from flying free.

"Rob?"

"Yeah?"

"If you *were* going to do it..."

"Shotgun. No note. Wouldn't say I was sorry at all."

I nodded and drank the last of my beer.

"You?" he asked.

I rested my head on his shoulder. "Same," I said. "Just the same."

Carlie St. George lives in Northern California, and may be a little strange. She works the night shift at a hospital, though, so this is only to be expected. She is also a Clarion West graduate, and her work has appeared in *Lightspeed* and *Weird Tales*. Her snarky movie reviews and other nerdy reflections can be found on her blog: mygeekblasphemy.com.

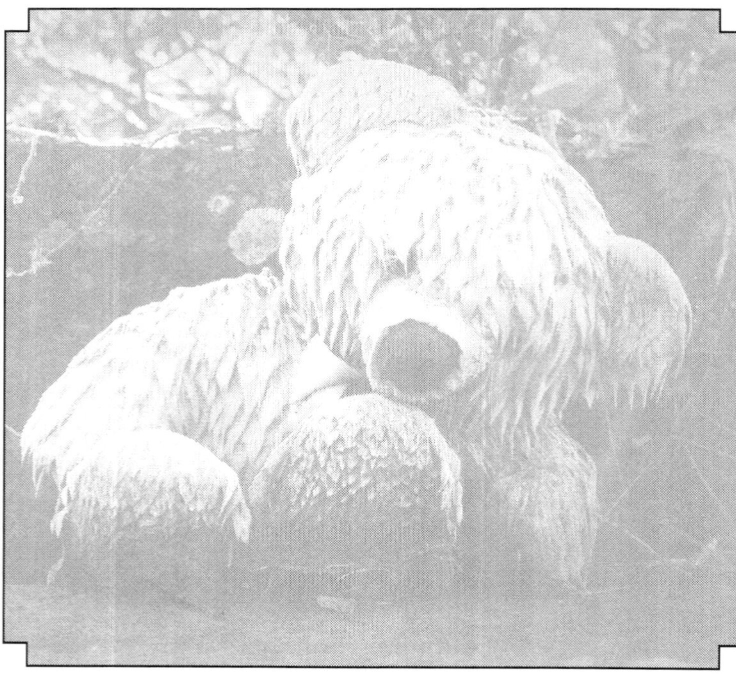

A Tale of True Horror
THE HIGHLAND LORD BROUGHT LOW

by Catherine Grant

That Easter morning in 1989, my brothers, Joe and Chris, had gone ahead to church with Aunt Linda, but I had stayed behind to ride with our parents, taking the extra time to make sure my Easter dress was perfect. Mom had let me pick it out a month prior at the department store—a pink-flowered frock of awkward length that looked like parlor curtains, with big, puffy sleeves and a bow in the back.

In my bedroom, I admired my reflection in the mirror. Satisfied, I then put on white socks bordered with lace and my new black leather shoes, and made my way downstairs, ready to twirl and show off my ensemble.

But I was met with silence.

My mother, also dressed for church, sat at the kitchen table, the blue sequins that dotted her sweater sparkling in the morning light. She crossed her legs, and I saw her chin quake. She frowned, lips pursed, and glanced toward the living room, where my father stood.

In his jeans and T-shirt, it was obvious he hadn't dressed for church. Before I could speculate as to what was going on, he yelled something unintelligible and, as I went to enter the kitchen, playfully wrestled me to the living-room couch, wrinkling my dress in the process. Back then Dad was still relatively healthy, a six foot, six inch Highland Lord, heavily muscled, raven-haired, and bearded. He knocked me over with little effort, and I looked up, annoyed, but quickly hid it out of instinct.

I was horrified his playfulness had mussed up my dress, but I tried to be a good sport. He *was* only trying to play with me, after all, and I forced a smile, wondering why he wanted to do this when we were supposed to be heading to church. I'd been waiting a month to show off my dress, and now we were going to miss the sunrise service. I regarded my mother, as I stood and faced the couch, but she didn't give any indication of what to do.

She looked away from me, toward my father. "We need to get to church, Steve."

Dad waved his hand, dismissing her. He was on his knees, the bulk of his body resting on the loveseat. He grabbed a brown stuffed bear off the floor. "Bite the bear before the bear bites you!" He stuck it in his mouth, shaking it back and forth like a dog.

I took a step away from him and giggled, even though I wasn't sure at all what he meant. I froze, watching him bite on the old stuffed animal, my smile fading. Even so young, I knew something was wrong. This wasn't his normal play, which was usually casual or even indifferent. He pulled the bear from his mouth.

Because he'd been chewing gum, the pink Bubblicious was stuck to the bear's fur.

"Oh well." He shrugged and tossed the stuffed animal over one shoulder, into the center of the living room.

My mother stood and padded over to where the bear lay. She bent down and picked it up, patting the stuffed animal with one hand, her jaw working back and forth when she saw the gum.

"You shouldn't treat this like it doesn't matter." She didn't look up. Her fingers picked at a spot on the bear's fur.

Dad shrugged. "I don't care."

She glared at him. "We got this on our honeymoon. Remember?"

He shrugged and Mom returned to the kitchen table, bear in hand.

Dad turned back to me. "Go upstairs and get my guitar. I want to play a song."

I was thankful to get away from him. Some of the tension in my shoulders dissolved as I climbed the stairs to the second floor and went into my parent's bedroom. I closed the door behind me, a flimsy barrier to whatever was going on below. The black guitar case lay on the floor like a casket. I popped the locks, and looked down at the cream-colored Ibanez that Dad had owned since I was an infant. I knew he couldn't really play, but I was going to bring it to him. I was afraid of what would happen if I didn't.

"Bring me my guitar, woman!" I heard him scream from below, almost on cue as I reached into the case.

Any thoughts of lingering in the room fled. Dad's tone was joking, but his words were cruel and distant, as though he didn't realize it was me at which he was flinging them. I took the guitar out of the case and cradled it like a baby downstairs and into the kitchen, where my father waited, sitting on a stool.

I handed him the Ibanez and he slipped the strap over his left shoulder. He began to strum, and from his fingers flew a cacophony of discord. He grinned, showing a mouth full of white teeth beneath his dark beard, and sang nonsense. It didn't sound like any song I knew, although at seven I'd been exposed to little more than New Kids on the Block and my mother's country music.

He stopped playing. "Wasn't that great?" He looked at me expectantly, and I nodded, giggling again to try to chase away the dead leaves of fear that were fluttering down, settling on my heart like a blanket. Dad pointed at a baseball resting on the floor. "Get that, I wanna play catch."

I nodded, retrieved the ball from the corner of the room, and brought it to him without question. He threw it to me, and I caught it deftly with one hand. I felt a bit giddy. We were playing ball in the house, something that my mother absolutely forbade. And we were doing it in front of her while she sat at the kitchen table.

I turned to her, and her face was like stone.

I tossed the ball back to my father. He caught it, spun quickly toward my mother, and shouted "Catch!" The baseball sailed through the air and fell heavy against the kitchen table, nearly hitting my mother in the face. The ball fell to the floor, hit the wall, and rolled back toward me.

He pointed and howled with laughter, not apologizing for the close call. "You were supposed to catch it," he barked.

I picked the ball up and clutched it in both of my small hands, not wanting to give it back to my father. I didn't want to play the game anymore.

"Stop it, Steve." My mother's voice was low, almost threatening.

"Why? We're just having fun."

She gestured toward me. "Can't you see that you're *scaring* her?"

My father frowned. "Am I scaring you?"

I didn't have to answer him. My mother's accusation felt like permission to break down. The question dissolved any scrap of strength I had left and I cried so hard that words would not visit my mouth, even to say "Yes" to my mother's question, as she expectantly looked at me, as if she hoped my display of fear would somehow stop the progression of my father's behavior. I nodded, to both of them, affirming that I didn't know what was going on and I was indeed scared.

My father's shoulders drooped and he scooped me up into his arms, giving me a good hug, telling me not to be afraid. He pulled back and smiled, and then asked me if I wanted another song. I shook my head and pulled away, looking toward my mother for rescue.

"Come on, Katie, we're going to church," she muttered, and stood from the table.

She took my hand, and led me out. We got into the car, a boat of a Cadillac, and I tried to enjoy the infrequent pleasure of sitting in the front seat. I smoothed out my wrinkled dress and dried my eyes. Not wanting to ask my mother the questions that crashed in on me with dark, half-hidden faces, I instead pushed them away, tucked them in for later, and turned to gaze out the window.

She dropped me off at the church with my brothers and aunt and went back home. I wandered alone through the gym that was decorated for Easter festivities, not caring about anyone seeing my dress, my joy at that small thing eclipsed by constant questions. I didn't want to participate in the Easter egg hunt, or Sunday school. I left the gym and went upstairs to one of the empty classrooms and curled up on the carpet, tracing the beige braids of the piling with one index finger as I replayed what my father had said over and over again in my mind. I came downstairs only when I heard the sounds of adults milling about in the lobby, a sure sign that service was over and that my mother would be back to pick us up soon.

But Mom never came. I rode in the front seat of my aunt's sedan and we went to her apartment. I didn't mention what had happened at the house earlier. I didn't want to know what was going on now. Later, when my brothers and I arrived back home, they asked pointedly where was Dad and why hadn't he been at church. My mother gathered us on the couch. We snuggled up, listening intently, while my youngest brother toddled on the floor at our feet.

"Dad is at the VA." I knew she meant the veteran's hospital, a place I remembered seeing often enough, although I hadn't made the connection as to why. "He'll be gone for a little while, okay? We can go visit him, though."

I nodded, and then Joe, who was turning five in a couple of weeks, asked if Dad would be home for his birthday. Mom said no, and the disappointment was immediate and terrible on Joe's face.

That night I knocked on my mother's door and asked if I could sleep with her. She obliged, reminding me as I climbed underneath the cold sheets not to move around a lot.

"Mom?"

She yawned. "Yes?"

"What happened to Dad?"

There was silence. I heard her sigh and saw the silhouette of her hand massage the bridge of her nose. "Your father is really sick." Then, a few moments later: "Katie, I'm sorry you had to see that."

I became lost in my own thoughts and didn't ask any more questions. Dad was sick, he went to a hospital, and that was all I needed to know.

Eventually, I slept.

Eight years later, my parents would get divorced, an absence that went on far longer than the few months Dad was at the VA. I had the choice to see him every other weekend, but I was old enough to decline, and so I did.

One day, when I was around eighteen, I received a phone call asking if I'd meet him at Dunkin' Donuts to talk things out. I pulled up in my beat-up Dodge Neon, expecting to see the raven-haired Lord I'd known as a child sitting in the dining room, sipping coffee. Instead, I saw an old man with silver hair and wrinkles. I saw a man with tattoos and a cane, clothes that had become too small and glasses that fell down his gaunt face. The change was startling from just a couple years earlier when he'd been removed, with police escort, from our home.

I sat down in front of him and the silence between us was a living thing, breathing and present. After a few moments, he broached the topic of why I hadn't come to see him and we were again the only two in the room.

"Because of what happened, while you were living with us," I said, trying not to sound so incredulous that he would even ask that.

He took a gulp of coffee—black, because that's how they had to drink it in Vietnam. No cream and sugar there. I remembered when he was living with us, bringing it to him by the gallon while he sat on his throne in the living room, just a beat-up computer chair with burns in the seat from when he fell asleep with a lit Pall Mall in his hand. He would do nothing but watch television for hours, or chat online with other "guitar players."

"Your mother poisoned you against me," he said. He was on lots of meds at that point: Oxycontin for the pain and a cocktail of anti-anxiety and anti-psychotic drugs. They kept him from cycling badly, but that was about it. "What did your mother tell you?"

I tried to look into his eyes and not to let the familiar mixture of love and resentment boil to the surface. I wanted to be calm for this. I looked into my cup instead and I remembered back to that Easter, when the reality of how mentally ill he was had crashed in to my little world. I repeated the mantra: *Dad is sick. I need to show understanding.* I tried to find that empathy within myself and scraped bottom.

"I don't need Mom to tell me anything," I said. "I was *there*. I heard the things you said and did."

I reminded him of a few examples. He didn't want to hear anymore.

Even after he shut down the conversation, I told him I'd come to the apartment on Thursdays, but I never did. I left Dunkin Donuts, and it would be the last time I'd see him. His phone calls went unanswered, and eventually I heard from my brothers that I'd been "cut off."

Three years later, I answered the phone call that my brothers and I had only the week prior speculated about receiving someday. The police were on the other line, asking for Mrs. Grant.

"I'm the only Mrs. Grant here," I said.

The officer hesitated. "I think I need to speak with your mother."

I knew what happened before she even came down the stairs, her expression full of the same conflicts I'd felt since I was a child—love and resentment, relief and guilt, peace and mourning. Dad had died. Because none of us were speaking to him at that time, he was alone and hadn't been found for three days. A friend who spoke to him regularly had suspected something was wrong and dialed the police. I called his friend before the funeral, to thank him.

"I came to visit your father about a month ago," he said. "We went to the movies and Outback. He bought a steak. It was like watching a king eat his last meal."

I visualized it, and wished I'd been there to say goodbye, even if I couldn't get the closure I wanted from him. I thanked his friend, the only person that had been left standing with my Dad in the end.

The funeral was in the morning, a modest event at the veteran's cemetery that my mother could barely afford. There was no funeral procession, no pomp or fanfare, no lengthy service. I read "Footprints in the Sand," the words choking in my throat halfway through. My Aunt Linda stepped forward to finish for me when it became obvious I couldn't move on. Afterward, she told me I was brave, a notion that I wanted to laugh at as my hands shook and I held in another round of sobs. The undertaker lowered my Dad's body into the ground among all the other soldiers, his grave marked by a white stone etched with his rank and title. It was not a funeral for a Highland Lord.

The family went to a restaurant after the service. I drank beer after beer until a numbness set in and I no longer wanted to cry. I tipped each glass skyward, sending a prayer to my father, hoping that wherever he was, he was finally at peace. I wished for that comfort as well.

I wanted peace for the twenty-one-year-old woman that was struggling with adulthood and all the choices that seemed insurmountable at times.

Most of all, I wished for reassurance for the seven-year-old girl in her Easter dress, twirling in the mirror and wanting nothing more than to show off her dress to her daddy. It was a simple love, one that I would do anything to get back again.

Catherine Grant lives in Connecticut with her cat/office assistant Miss Mau. She is an office monkey for a Connecticut mental health and addictions non-profit, freelance journalist, bibliophile, gamer and connoisseur of caffeine-laden beverages.

Swearing At the Dinner Table
A Conversation with Cody Goodfellow

by John Boden

There is bizarro...then there is what Cody Goodfellow does. His material is just as brazen and off-kilter as the wildest of Bizarros, but there is an arcane logic to his proceedings. A slithering and cold calculation to the goings-on and characters that populate his tales. It isn't just *Hey, this guy wakes up with a hamster head and has to save his girlfriend from alien blender maniacs.* His is a style shrewd and steeped in science and dark arts. But rest assured there is no shortage of gore and goo.

Cody was kind enough to stop by the manor and sit for a fine brunch of stale cheetos and lemonade.

~

JB: I first heard of you through the notorious John Skipp interview I conducted for *Shock Totem #1*. The result of nearly four hours of phone chat with the excitable man. You were mentioned as a new voice he was excited about *and* as the current collaborative partner he had. So I noted the books he spoke of and tracked them down. I have to say, I have never read anything quite like your work. It's like 80s splatter punk with a strange Cronenbergian body-horror element thrown in. That and just a lot of weird. I loved it. Did you find it difficult finding a home for your work before the burgeoning acceptance of bizarro? I'd think "traditional" markets would have pissed their pants at the thought.

CG: Bizarro is burgeoning, but I wouldn't say there's been a lot of acceptance... It still gets disrespected pretty much throughout the rest of the horror ghetto, and the sci-fi and fantasy people are like the squares in *Caddyshack* when the Bizarros jump in the pool. I've seen more "mature" writers who are always sloshy drunk in the daytime take them to task for dressing unprofessionally, and I've heard miserable, bitter aging writers who will die unread railing against how their vulgarity makes the genre look bad.

(What was the...? oh yeah...)

It was murder trying to find markets that would read me at all when I was earnestly trying to fit in coming up, but I figured it was the same for everybody. I didn't get much useful feedback, so it wasn't for quite a while that I began to realize there was anything weird, really, about my work. I was laboring under the presumption that the genre should continue to surprise, shock and stun, so I was trying to find subjects and themes and ideas that hadn't been hacked to death. If it's stopped being scary or mysterious and you're still revisiting it, it isn't horror; it's comfort food, or porn.

I made a lot of friends in the horror community, but my work isn't what most people think of as horror, because most people define horror the way you'd define a western, with a checklist of things. Horror is less a genre than an emotion, every sensible book on writing the stuff tells you, but if it has no slashers, zombies, evil children, haunted houses or ancient evil appearing to fuck with a writer returning to his small hometown, it seems to miss the bus. The New Weird thing seemed promising at first, but it's too self-consciously formalistic for me. I can appreciate sophisticated entertainment and criticism, but I love art that picks its nose and swears at the dinner table and isn't afraid of what it is.

Until Jeremy Robert Johnson invited me to put out my books through his Swallowdown imprint, I didn't feel like a bizarro writer; I was just content to hang out and drink their beer. I still don't think my work sits comfortably in the bizarro frame, now that it's become an established subgenre, if not a formula. I try to take something really weird and make it as real and relatable as possible, whereas bizarro, boiled down to an imitable brand, mutates very universal humanistic themes by throwing in all kinds of absurdism and pop culture and cartoonish filters. In a broader sense, though, where bizarro is simply storytelling that fundamentally inverts or subverts the reader's basic expectations, I think I fit in quite snugly. One of my earliest coherent memories is getting in trouble for loudly denying the existence of God and Santa Claus in a mall at Xmas, so it follows that everything I do is in some way to shake people out of their false contentment. Hanging out with the Bizarros has rubbed off on me, certainly. My readings get more ridiculous every time I go out. I'm trying to rehabilitate the subversive discourse of prop comedy.

JB: I started with the *Radiant Dawn* and *Ravenous Dusk*, in regard to your solo work. And I was blown away. It was a great big gory crash scene of government conspiracy, mutation, and cultish boogeda boogeda. From there, I picked up your short-story collection, *Silent Weapons for Quiet Wars*, and that thing is built of brilliant. The opener, "Baby Teeth," sets up the ride perfectly. Where do these ideas come from?

CG: Everywhere. I am motivated to write more by fascination than fear, and I've trained my brain to vivisect everything in my world that gives me even a fleeting spark of intrigue. You have to interrogate everything, letting it rattle around like the contents of a rock tumbler, until it reveals what's so compelling about itself... or at least falls into some narrative that lets the mystery take on a life of its own.

I threw everything at *Radiant Dawn* that I had in me, proceeding from the assumption that I probably wasn't going to write another book. I'd had some rotten experiences in publishing that made me bitter and mistrustful of everyone, and so those books were going to be something of a declaration of war on everything I thought the people who weren't giving me a chance were doing wrong.

And the worst possible thing happened. Only a few people found it, but they loved it. So we had to do the sequel, which still didn't get reviewed anywhere or garner any attention within or without the genre. So I broke down and started going to cons and meeting people. And the first person I met was Skipp.

My short fiction is weird to me, because I couldn't write decent shorts or even plot them, until after I'd done the novels. Now, some are years-long projects while others fall off the brow like sweat. But I'm terribly proud of that collection. Some of my newest stuff is in there with some of my first stories, and it seems to hit emotional registers I wasn't aiming for, consciously.

"Baby Teeth," for instance, just distills a bunch of autobiographical stuff. I come from hoarders, and we keep everything. My brother was just finishing high school and being a prick, and my daughter had finished losing her milk teeth and I had them all in this little sack and I put them in a Camel tin in which I stored my step-grandmother's false teeth, which is another story… But just trying to find a metaphor for that compulsion to cling to the evidence, relics and trash, of the past. And so there's a lot in there that's intensely personal, but sublimated and stitched together into a scarecrow wearing odds and ends of mine, and stuff I stole off other people's lives.

JB: You've collaborated with Skipp on at least three books now. What is it like working with a man who is as hyper as a ten-year-old high on Pepsi and Sweet Tarts? I cannot imagine the idea sessions you two must have. You're imagination seems to be as feral and out there as his. I'd wager it's like living Rock'em Sock'em Robots.

CG: He's the calm one, most days. I'm a lot more pessimistic, but we egg each other on nicely. Working together is a ton of fun. It has to be, when it's something you both could be doing alone. It's more like air guitar dueling on trampolines than boxing.

We've figured out how to divide labor according to our strengths and do our parts and then put it together pretty seamlessly. It helps that we both do music. Before we wrote anything together, we goofed around and made some songs, and that model has informed all our collaborations. You harmonize and you break into solos and just use the other guy's variations to bring out new wrinkles in your own stuff. I love the solitude of writing, but eventually I get fed up with my own rhythms, my favored vocabulary, my pet ideas. Skipp puts surprise and a sense of play back into the work.

JB: What or who, are some of your influences? I hear you carry a torch for that Lovecraft feller, but there is also an obvious cinematic vibe to your work, so I would assume a hefty presence of directors also play a part.

CG: I still live deep in Lovecraft country, and I like writing CAS pastiches and cheesy pulp adventure à la REH. But my "real" style, the voice in my head, came from studying cyberpunk writers like Gibson and Shirley and Rucker and maximalists like Pynchon and DeLillo. The morality in my stories, too, I draw more from science fiction than from horror. Good and evil are not just unrealistic, they're lazy.

I've been reading more crime lately…not so much to write it as to pick up some skills at economizing. Everyone knows, or think they know, what they're getting into with a crime story, so you're freed from a lot of exposition. Bringing more of that into horror would be a great gift to a genre that still believes people want epic, heavily padded novels.

I grew up thinking I was going to write films, but undergraduate school in LA in the period when all the studios were being taken over and restructured as vertically integrated corporations cured me of that. But film still informs my work more than it should. My favorite movies all came out in the summer of '82. I love Cronenberg and took more than just ideas from his films; his genius for articulating visceral obsession is something I've tried to reproduce in my own work.

The speed and immediacy of film made horror exciting again when the splatterpunks brought it back to the page, but it also left behind a lot of the techniques that make prose more psychologically powerful even than film. I'm slowly trying to inject more sensory data than just sight and sound into my writing and to make it feel more like writing, or a transparent dream, and less like a treatment for an unfilmable film.

JB: See, I *knew* there had to be enormous Cronenberg influence on you. Do you read a lot? How important is what you read and its shading of what you write? There is heavy political allegory in quite a bit of your work. Do you follow the goings on in the political arena? That shit is far more terrifying these days than anything a writer could conjure up.

CG: I read constantly but slowly, and I do absorb tone from everything I read.

Rather than cut myself off, I read the kind of things that exemplify the kind of voice I'm going for. I'm doing a horror crime book right now, so I've been reading a lot of noir and crime stuff; but I'm also doing a comic book about artificial meat, so I have to freebase mass quantities of hideous anecdotes about industrial slaughterhouses. Weird random things I throw in usually percolate up in some unpredictable way.

I follow politics avidly, and use it to get pissed off every morning, but rather than go out looking for Facebook fights, I try to channel that anger back into my writing. I don't feel the need to lay down my political beliefs in public and alienate half my audience, when I could potentially get them to pay me to challenge everything they believe in a novel. Before I even followed politics, I read Ellison's Gentleman Junkie, and it made me seethe about racism and anti-Semitism and payola in rock radio, and I realized this was a way of pumping out your anger like venom from a wound, and then selling the stuff.

JB: How much and where does music fit in with your creative process? I recall the answer to an interview I read with you a few years ago, where you were asked about going back in time to be a roadie for anyone. You had mentioned Skinny Puppy, Ministry, and Metallica in your answer…and my heart warmed. We love music at Shock Totem, all sorts of styles…so wow us with your digs!

CG: I love music at least as much as I love writing, and more often, I feel it loves me back. I use it to stay inside a story for as long as possible, and when I'm burned out on words, I go poke out some half-assed homebrew techno and it restores my faith in the mysteries of the creative process. All too much about writing is deliberate for me, but composing anything is an experiment, because I don't know what the fuck I'm doing.

I listen to almost everything that has no vocals in it. I used to audit alternative rock radio for ten years, identifying artists and song titles, and so I got burned out on rock and fed up with singing and lyrics. It's always a story or a voice that plugs you into a situation or an emotional state, where instrumental music opens up the mind and lets you explore your own stories.

I've always loved industrial but as my arteries have hardened I've drifted more towards dub, vintage exotica and ambient electronica. My favorite spins while I'm writing these days are Amon Tobin, Broken Note, Shpongle, Ott, Mauxuam, Martin Denny, Secret Chiefs 3, the Orb, and lots of spy music on Soma.fm. In the car this summer, I've been playing Queens of the Stone Age, Mr. Bungle, Ratatat, Grimes, Wall of Voodoo, Yeasayer, and Major Lazer, but when I'm stuck in traffic I crank up whatever's on the classical station and make O-faces at strangers until they let me cut them off.

I once got to interview John Balance from Coil, one of my favorite groups, and one that felt somehow uniquely mine because I'd only ever met a handful of people who'd ever heard of them. Their stuff is sinister beyond all reason; they did a soundtrack for Hellraiser that was deemed too creepy to use in the film. Anyway, I asked him about the bizarre subjects for their songs and how they evoke such a pervasively weird and malevolent atmosphere on tape. I thought I was paying him a compliment, but he just sighed and said, "We're not trying to be strange. We're just trying to communicate sincerely about the things that we love."

And ever since then, that's all I've ever tried to do, too.

JB: That's actually a pretty good standard to go by. What is coming up on the Goodfellow horizon? New collaborativeness with Skipp? Film? Taxidermied sculpture?

CG: I'm trying to fight my way back to the next novel, but the short story work I would've loved to have ten years ago is burying me. Skipp and I are slated to take on a major genre nonfiction project next year, and hopefully my next novel, *Repo Shark*, will be out from Swallowdown in time for Xmas. It's about a repo man who goes to Hawaii to take a vintage Harley back from a were-shark.

JB: Holy hell! That sounds great! I'd like to thank you for chatting with me. As I said I am a big fan of your work, and one of the coolest things Shock Totem has afforded me, is the chance to chat with people I dig and who have inspired me. Any final outbursts or remarks before we adjourn?

CG: Sure...

When I was researching the meatpacking industry, I learned that chickens, who are prone to cannibalism anyway, will often set upon each other with a vengeance when they're packed up on the truck bound for the slaughterhouse, many even after they've been debeaked. Now, as I so often do when I come across some startling truth about the animal kingdom, I reflexively pictured human beings doing the same thing. And in this case, I couldn't imagine humans pecking each other to death even as they're all being carted off to a plucking and certain doom... not until the next time I clicked over to Facebook.

Much as it delights me to see so many of my peers frolicking in the tar pits of social media and thinking they're being writers, it drives me up the fucking wall to see so much energy wasted in miscommunication, in outrage orgies and petty arguments that seem to scratch the creative itch for so many self-professed artists. Half of it is assholes flying their asshole flag and professing shock to discover they're being called on it. But fewer and fewer of even the slender percentage of reasonable people out there seem to grasp the differences between fact and opinion, between criticism and hatred and censorship.

I see amateurs and semi-pros shouting past each other, thinking they're debating when they're just beating crudely assembled straw men. I more or less withdrew from social media when every argument ended up detouring into willful misunderstanding and having to clarify and repeat just what you'd said and why. As a writer, your art is effective communication. The foundation of the craft is leaving no wiggle room for interpretation of what you set down.

Some of it is the decline of logic itself, but a lot more of it is people are angry because they believe they've done all the work and the audiences they've been told to expect just aren't showing up; or the audience that shows up is just there to sell their own books… and it's somehow not enough to have the gift of being able to express something in words that someone else will pay for, if someone else is making a living at it.

Now more than ever, nobody's getting the kind of validation they need from this thing of ours, but even people who try to jokingly redefine what professionalism means to include these strugglers on the margins who sincerely are trying to say something in a compelling, entertaining, artful way are getting shit on, because the fighting…

I think even the fighting with other writers is less frightening than the silence and the solitude of actually writing. I think a lot of the noise cluttering up the social scenes of the various genre ghettos is the end product of people being afraid to be alone with their own heads. You can't entertain yourself so you close your work in progress and go over to Facebook and Holy shit, can you believe what that idiot said? And even the ugliest scene one can get embroiled in is going to be easier than facing that you just can't entertain yourself, so how can you expect to entertain anyone else?

When William Lee offers someone his old typewriter in Cronenberg's *Naked Lunch*, he says it produces several different types of hallucinogenic substance when it likes what you've written, he wasn't talking about a typewriter or even drugs. He was talking about his brain. I think I'm only able to get more written on the page than on blogs or Facebook, to write instead of being a writer, because I genuinely enjoy the solitude. I live to entertain myself. And I'm blessed with a brain with an easily jimmied medicine chest.

JB: That is actually fairly spot on. There is a reason I rarely engage in anything deeper than a plug for Shock Totem-related things or my own writing and music videos. Opinions are wielded like nail-studded baseball bats…and no

one gets it when you try to bring that to light. I'll leave this as it stands. Thanks again.

CG: Thanks, this was a lot of fun!

The Barham Offramp Playhouse

by Cody Goodfellow

When everybody stops showing up to an acting class in Hollywood, it's for one of three reasons. A new and edgier method group has sprung up; a big in-town feature is casting extras; or Randy Hurlburt killed the vibe one too many times, and everyone bailed.

Though he'd be the first to admit he was kind of slow, Randy was not totally oblivious to this phenomenon. Even if he couldn't acknowledge it, he knew at some bone-deep level that he sucked the life out of a room. So when he ran into three of the old NoHo Free Theater improv gang at the El Coyote, he played it cool. He'd already hit two workshops this week that had mysteriously vaporized.

He knew something was wrong when one of them spotted him and called him over. "Hey, look, Randy's here!" Jerry Aziz's laugh sounded like cheap breakaway glass. "Now it's a party, right?" The other three in the booth stared lazy daggers at him, but they scooted over.

Sheila had been around since long before Randy came to town, and she was Randy's first celebrity acquaintance; he recognized her from the old Clapper ads. Even for Hollywood, she was a mean person. Tammy was a second-string porn starlet, but heeded the call to pursue legitimate acting when her triple-D implants ruptured. Nodules of free-floating silicone still swam around loose under her skin. Colin was allegedly a certified Lee Strasberg instructor, but he couldn't hold a class together. He kept going to workshops to harass other acting coaches and pick up on younger, dumber men.

Jerry was a dental hygienist. He had twice played dentists on TV shows nobody saw, and once, in a bold reach, he'd played a pharmacist with one line on one of those shows on TNT with all the swears.

"Hey, you guys," Randy mumbled, trying to low-ball their apathy. Each was nursing a birdbath-sized pomegranate margarita. He started to tell them about his day, his week, his larger strategy, but they closed up. They didn't even laugh at his report on the student zombie film in which he was an extra. They charged him eighty bucks to be in it, even though he did his own makeup.

"That's awesome, Randy," Colin said, "but the grownups are still talking." He sucked his electric cigarette until the little LED cherry made like a red strobe. "You're not going down there, Jerry. It's fucking suicide. Literally *and* socially."

"You're just scared because it's *real*," Aziz shouted, looking around the cantina, but the waitresses were old hands at ignoring hammy scenes. "I'm going. You poseurs can come with me and try something *real*, or at least come support me, or you can all fuck off."

"You're not going through with it," Tammy pouted. Her upper lip plumped like a burst bicycle tire. "And you don't have the physicality for it. Not for any of the really *real* parts—"

"*You* know about it?" Colin banged his fake cig on the table. "Does *every* loser in the Valley know about it?"

"What're you guys talking about?" Randy asked, but he was sure they wouldn't tell him.

Something *real*.

Tomorrow, whatever it was would be all the rage, and everyone would be talking about it, trying to cop a feel off it until they smothered it.

They all just looked at him like he was made out of bugs. Even Aziz regretted calling him over. "We're talking about going...somewhere new," he mumbled.

"*We're* not going anywhere," Colin said. His voice went up an octave like a slutty coed in a slasher movie.

"*I* want to go," Randy said, totally swept away in the moment. He'd only come in looking for leads on audition call-ups or to fish for some positive reinforcement to get back into workshops. "I want to try out, too, man, for... whatever."

Aziz looked around the table. Sheila and Tammy were studiously texting each other. Colin shook his head and called for the check.

"Fine," Jerry said, "fuck you all very much. I'll just go with *Randy*, then."

He turned to Randy and grabbed the bigger man's biceps to yank him down until they almost knocked heads as he towed him out of El Coyote. "You want to come with me, then all you have to do is shut the fuck up. We're not going to a class or a workshop or an audition. Where we're going, I'm not going to try to explain right here, but it needs an audience, so you can come. And if you're not too careful, you might just learn everything there is to know about acting, tonight."

~

Randy believed he already knew everything there was to acting, and it hadn't helped. He'd been knocking around Hollywood for almost eleven years. He knew everybody who wasn't making it. And from Day One, people had been telling him to shut the fuck up and listen.

As a serious actor, he knew you had to make a constant study of people. You had to shut up and listen, observe and learn to get inside their heads and hearts. It was a difficult discipline to master, but in ten years of listening, Randy had heard almost nothing but other actors talking about acting.

When he first dropped out of high school and came out from Tucson, Randy had hit every audition with vigor and panache, left everyone remembering his name. He had been summoned into the limelight with a born-again ferocity, and went everywhere to spread the gospel of himself. The casting agents called him Randy The Barbarian, goofed on him and made small talk with him like old classmates, but they never, ever gave him work. He had "boundless enthusiasm and a distinctive, goonish, look," but he needed polish. They all had friends who ran excellent acting workshops.

But the heavenly limelight that bewitched him had proved to be a bug zapper. He had accumulated forty-eight extra roles on various basic cable cop shows, and been dropped by almost as many agents. He had a trunk full of costumes that he donned to pose for pictures in front of the Mann Chinese at the end of the month to make rent on his studio in North Hollywood. None of the costumes fit anymore, and now he and his arthritic Great Dane, Conan, lived in his van.

Somewhere along the line, it had stopped being anything like fun or even a way to earn a living, and had become a religion. He had dedicated his life to the Big Break, and so It Must Come. What else was he wired for?

At least he wasn't alone, even if it always felt that way. Aziz barely talked to him as they drove north up Cahuenga. The major boulevard turned into a two-lane game trail squashed against the crumbling sandstone cliffs by the mighty concrete anaconda of the 101. The eight-lane freeway was choking on its dinner, and they blew by the traffic on the frontage road.

"Come on, Jerry, baconberryfatsofairy," Randy needled. "Where we going?"

Aziz bit his lip, working out his motivation. "What did you want, when you first came to this town, Randy?"

"Shit, man, I want—"

"To be famous? Rich? Powerful? Loved?"

"All of the above, dude..."

"No. What did you *need*, to feel complete?"

Randy picked up Aziz's cue that this was a serious question, and not a rhetorical one. He'd heard this kind of stuff before from frustrated actors. This was the kingdom of dreams, and a dream was a wish, not a promise.

"Jerry my brother," he began a hell of a soliloquy...

Aziz cut him off. "I just wanted to be somebody else, you know? Anybody else..."

Someone swerved in front of them, cutting them off without realizing they were there, and Aziz waved his hand, grateful for the illustration. "This city is a sinkhole of selfishness. Every negative has a positive, right? You'd think there must be a city on the exact opposite of the globe from LA, where nobody ever lies, and the ideal is total negation of the self, where everyone looks after everyone else..."

And everybody stands on their heads and eats shit and poops bread, right? They're still humans, so they probably fall all over themselves trying to have nothing at all, and they're still not happy. All of this came into Randy's head too fast to make it out of his mouth, so he just said, "We *are* on the other side of the world from LA. Welcome to the Valley."

Beyond the saddle of Cahuenga Pass, the rugged mountain terrain surrendered to Hollywood's seedy evil twin, North Hollywood. The gyms, pawnshops, fast food joints, temples and porno studios had none of old Hollywood's mystique or glamour, but over here, shit got done on time and under budget. Every blowjob was on the clock.

Jerry said, "You know anything about voodoo?"

"Like with the dolls and the shrunken heads? I'm hip, man, but...are you, like, into that shit?"

"No, God..." Sucking his painfully well-maintained grill, Jerry tried again. "You know how they dance around, drunk off their asses and make offerings to the gods and stuff, just so the gods will come down and take over their bodies?"

"I guess..."

"Well, what do you think it was like, the first time it happened? Before it became a religion, something they tried to make happen every full moon, or whatever? All those clowns pretending they're getting possessed, it's just acting, even if—no, especially if—they believe it's really happening. But what if it really *is* happening?"

Aziz parked in a minimall lot on Cahuenga and Barham, in front of the Universal Psychic. He turned and looked at Randy like he was about to lay down some serious expository dump on his head...but then he just sighed and got out.

Randy trotted after him. Did he lock his car? Randy was nervous, and nerves made him hungry. "Hey, dude, you want to get a burger at the In N Out, after?"

"Come on, goddammit!" Aziz crossed the parking lot and turned onto the Barham Avenue overpass. The elegant New Deal-era bridge over the 101 looked like a relic from a bygone species next to all the pre-fab, Lego-block construction around it. There was nothing on the other side of the bridge but a few drab apartments, an auto body place and a casting office, unless you drove up the hill to Universal Studios and Citywalk, or over it to Forest Lawn.

Colin's crack about suicide replayed in his head. Jerry did seem pretty depressed, but who didn't? "Hey, man, whatever it is, it's not worth it!"

Aziz stopped in mid-span, hacking up a lung, then lighting up an unfiltered Camel. "What, you thought I was coming up here to *jump?*" Aziz sucked half the cigarette down and looked out over the ballistic post-rush hour traffic.

The old northbound Barham offramp was closed down about ten years ago. Less than fifty yards long, one lane wide and steeply turning onto the Universal Studios driveway, Barham was a deathtrap for today's speedfreak, phone-equipped suburban tanks, and in rush hour, the line to exit always backed up traffic halfway to downtown, so the city shut it down. As vital an exit as it was, its central location, surrounded by valuable real estate and the car-clogged aorta of Hollywood, made it impossible to seriously renovate, and so the orphan offramp persisted as an unintentional landmark.

Randy went to the edge of the bridge and looked over the railing. "Whoa, how did that get there?"

At the foot of the condemned offramp, there sat a house. Perched on the shoulder overlooking the freeway, silhouetted against the flurry of headlights and the blue neon miasma of the Vivid Video headquarters, it looked like a repossessed

American Gothic farmhouse.

From above, in the sickly greenish highway lights, the shingled roof looked like the scaly hide of a long-dead dragon, sagging between crooked rafters and drooping over the eaves as if it was beginning to melt.

Aziz waved at Randy and then, at a break in the traffic on the overpass, he hopped the chainlink fence and ran down the offramp, stooped over like a bad SWAT team extra. Randy followed.

The house was a white early 20th century blue-collar bungalow with a porch and gable windows and a brick chimney—hardly out of place in Los Angeles, but way out of place up on blocks on the shoulder of the 101.

Nobody knew where it came from. It was just sitting there about a week ago, when morning rush hour broke. It was the only logical place in the area to dump something of its size if there were problems with the trailer, and nobody in the city had taken much trouble to do anything about it, beyond putting cones around it and a sign on the back so motorists would stop parking behind it and honking.

A few hastily scrawled graffiti tags—CHAKA IV – DOGNOGGIN – MOEBIUS DICK—marked the side of the house facing the retaining wall. They were so sloppy and rushed, it looked like just touching the house at all was some kind of badge of courage.

Jerry Aziz hopped the fence and the barricades at the foot of the aborted offramp. Randy caught up with him and grabbed his arm. "Wait up, man. What could possibly be down there—"

Aziz whipped around and shoved Randy away. For just a moment, he looked crazy enough to throw himself into traffic, and reminding him that it wasn't moving fast enough to kill him anyway didn't seem like the way to calm him down. "Get off me, you fucking lummox! I'm not trying to off myself. I gotta get in, before they cast everybody. You can come with me or not, but don't get in my way. I've *earned* this."

Randy let him go, but following him was much harder. This place was dangerous, and what was the payoff? A house dropped like junk by the side of the road. Jerry was consumed by it, the others were afraid of it. Randy's own fear was dwarfed by his all-consuming phobia of missing out.

The house rested uneasily on some sort of block and tackle set up four feet off the tarmac. Jerry was too short to hop up onto the porch. It was almost funny, watching the little guy hop and curse. The lowest step crumbled under his feet and fell off, shedding fairy dust sprinkles of termite shit on the hot car exhaust wind. Feeling a surge of panic as headlights speared them like prison searchlights, Randy gave him a boost onto the porch.

The doors and windows were boarded up, but the plywood over the front door had been wrenched halfway off. Crushed cigs and glittering emerald bits of glass covered the scuffed, whitewash boards.

Jerry pried the doorway open and slid inside. Randy looked around, fully expecting the headlights to turn red and blue and start screaming at him. The plywood came off in his hands, but he laid it back over the open door and sealed himself up inside the house.

It was dark, stuffy and stale inside. Quiet, but not silent. Still, but hardly empty.

He heard voices, strident and loud, from somewhere in the house. And cheers and applause.

Randy forgot his fear and fumbled down the hall. At last, he'd found the underground.

Candlelight leaked into the hall, illuminating rounded archways and cracked molded ceilings draped with huge capes of dingy cobweb. Ducking under them, he stuck his head into the dining room and immediately flattened against the wall.

What the hell…?

The room was packed with people. He recognized a lot of them from workshops, but the rest were a weird mix of hipsters, freaks and the homeless. They sat on the floor or leaned against the wall, utterly rapt and wide-eyed, somewhere between children at a magic show and fiends watching somebody chop out coke lines.

A family sat at the dinner table, heads bowed over plates with pork chops and potatoes. Nobody moved. Nobody breathed. Were they mannequins?

He figured this must be some kind of guerilla version of those interactive dinner theater things that were all the rage when he first came to town, but the heavy pall of pregnant silence that sat on the room was not of the theater. It felt more like a séance.

At the head of the table, the father lowered his steepled hands and looked into the faces of his family. His brutish, ruddy face cracked like drying mud.

His wife kept her praying hands up in defense. Behind them, her face was a gray mask, colored only by bruises. His daughters, one a slender but plain teen, the other no more than ten or twelve, hunched their shoulders and prayed harder.

"Let us give thanks," the father said. "Tonight, we'll go around the table, and see what everyone's thankful for. Mother, you start."

"I'm…I…" the mother stuttered, "I am grateful for this meal…"

"Did God do that for you, or did I?"

"I—I—I…made the meal, but…"

Father shook his head ruefully and punched her in the mouth. "Nadine, pick it up."

Without looking up from the church of her hands, the older sister answered, "I'm thankful for Daddy's strength," she said.

Father smiled and hacked at his pork chop. "That's nice, baby girl. And what strength is that?"

"Our Daddy's strong, and he'll take care of us, no matter what."

"That's right, baby girl. I wish those cocksuckers at the plant saw it clear the way you do. Trudy?"

The little girl poked the creamed corn over to the edge of her plate. "I wish to God that Tim would come back."

"I don't think I heard you right." Father dropped his knife and fork. "I don't rightly know anybody by that name. Mother, do you?"

Mother shook her head so hard it almost came unscrewed.

Nadine put her arm around Trudy. "Oh Daddy, she's just talking about her old kitten..."

"Really, darlin'? Is that what you meant?"

The whole room trembled as the audience forgot to breathe.

"I just miss him, that's all."

"Well..." Father pushed his plate away. "Maybe you just do. And maybe you just forgot who it is, that hears prayers and makes miracles happen around here. Maybe you forgot who giveth and who taketh away in this house." Father snatched up his plate and flung it at Trudy like a Frisbee.

The little girl ducked and the plate sailed over the audience's heads to smash into the far wall. A few giggled, and were dutifully shushed.

"Daddy, please don't—"

Father stood up. A big, barrel-chested working man, his fists were bigger than his youngest child's head. When he brought them down on the table, the plates danced. Milk glasses toppled. "Maybe the whole world's forgotten what a man is worth, and maybe he don't amount to much out there, but in *here*, a man is still king of his castle, and his word is law. And...and..."

Father gripped his chest. His eyes bugged out and a little string of bile erupted from his tightly clamped mouth. "I'm okay...I can do it..."

"CUT!" A short man with tall, bleached-blonde hair leapt out of the front row and rushed the table. "You." He pointed at the father. "Get out."

The father sat back down in his chair, hyperventilating, shrinking. Now, he was just a lanky bald guy in a spangled Ed Hardy T-shirt. Randy rubbed his eyes and stared. Was it magic? Or was it acting?

Randy knew better than to blunder into the room asking people what was going on, so he just crept back through the crowd until he found a vacant patch of wall.

He stood there looking at the table until a stunning redhead whispered in his ear, "You don't belong here."

"Sure I do," he hissed back. "I came with my friend." He pointed at Jerry. He burned to chat her up, but he knew better, so he shut up and listened as she told some guy who looked like a fit model for International Male.

The house came from Fontana, where it'd sat empty after the family—

"Spoiler alert," a hipster with one of those Arab terrorist scarves cut in.

The most popular rumor went that the father killed the whole family, right here in this room. Some rich ghoul bought the house and was moving it, when it fell off the truck. A couple taggers went into the house the first night, and discovered that the dead people in the house wanted to talk. Every night since then, a growing group of actors, artists and seekers had come to play out the scene.

It was the ultimate improv game. When the actors really got into the characters, they disappeared into them, but like any scene, it was already starting to drown in its own audience.

"It's still pretty awesome," the redhead said, "but the ending is kind of fucked up. The whole thing kind of breaks down, when he kills them all, and then kills himself."

"Actually," the hipster corrected, "It's not the same thing every night. Last night, the mother turned the tables on him and cut his head off." When the conversation stalled, he added, "I mean, not for real...I don't think...but it was *awesome*."

The director got volunteers from the audience to carry the actor who played the father out. The mother and daughters sat hyperventilating, floppy and used-up and ecstatic like pilgrims touched by a faith healer. The mother's nose was crooked and dripping blood freely onto her plate.

"We need a new father," the director said, lighting a cigarette. "Quickly, who's ready, who's *feeling* it?"

Jerry Aziz jumped up with the others in the front row. Randy got up but didn't play eager. Emote at the director from across the room. Feel that hot spot on the back of your neck? That's *me*.

"You," the director jabbed his nose at a mountainous lesbian with a grown-out Mohawk in the back of the room. "You were born to be the Daddy." The dyke crushed an empty beercan and mowed down a path to the table.

And you," he added, pointing at Trudy. "Out. That plate was supposed to hit you in the face. Trudy *wants* to be punished. I need somebody who can pick up what this fucking space is putting down. Someone who will really get lost in the role and show us what *really* happened. Anyone? No...You? No...Anyone...? *You*."

Randy thought the finger was on him and rushed the table pumping his fist like a boss, which made the group laugh. The director brushed him aside and tapped Jerry on the head. Jerry smiled at the brief splatter of applause, and took his place in the little girl's chair.

Randy took a bow. The audience deflated, venting contempt. Hands grabbed his arms and legs and passed him, bucket-brigade style, to the far corner of the room.

There was nothing for him here. Nothing to learn, no chance to shine. His first acting coach was right. *You can't polish a turd*.

Exit, stage left. Don't come back. Get a real job. Get real friends, start dating again.

Don't let the dream die—kill it with your bare hands.

He shrank along the wall to the hallway, still festooned with broken ribbons of CAUTION tape.

That was it, then. The grave was so wide he couldn't see the other side of it.

The grave was so deep his whole life fit into it with plenty of room for a dismal, savagely truncated future.

Down the hall he wandered, sinking into the mildewed plaster and starting to feel like he was going to cry. Behind him, the crowd fell silent, the actors opening themselves up to the vibe of the house, or some other method technique.

Bullshit. Actor as psychopomp. Spirits, what's my motivation? Let's solve a murder with our ART! Fuckfuckfuck you. Fuck you all.

Feel better now? No, he didn't. But now he didn't fear feeling empty.

And into his emptiness, there flowed...everything.

If these walls could talk...they wouldn't. They'd just scream. He could hear them in the fillings in his teeth, so loud and so shrill that he lashed out and punched them. His fist went through tarpaper and studs like stale bread. The coffin-shaped space inside the walls the reeked of mouse turds and dust and flop sweat and hungry breath, and it was stuffed with the brittle yellow pages of *Variety* and *Playbill*.

Nobody was ever murdered here. It didn't take a murder to make a ghost. This house had become like a toxic waste dump—or a storage battery. The bad shit had to go to ground and saturated the termite-riddled wood and sagging plaster. The ground where it had sat probably had been fenced off and slowly reclaimed over years, like when they shut down his dad's gas station.

Randy stumbled down the hall into the bathroom. Flipped up the lid and stooped to puke. The amputated drain opened on the grooved freeway pavement below. Scattered flashes of car headlights shone up at him. Wiping his mouth he looked around. Peeling and water-stained, but the remnants of posters on walls and ceiling were easier to read.

The flow was overwhelming back here, away from the crowd, the echoes of suffering and ecstasy and death, death DEATH in Shakespearean quality and Peckinpah quantity. But where every other actor in this impromptu troupe had snatched a mask out of the rushing whirlpool of phantoms that swarmed this place, Randy just watched them flow by until they repeated themselves and he saw through it all to the eye, to the heart, to the truth of the mystery.

Well, he thought, *that fucking figures*.

Nobody died here, he thought, and all of them died here, every night. The father killed them every night with his disapproval and endless demands and scenes, endless melodramatic improv exercises. The daughters, the mother barely had personalities of their own, and the son...the empty chair at the table, the one nobody could play and so he was simply written out of the shambling séance scene in the dining room. Their scene was going nowhere and doing nothing, because the one voice that could end it was silent.

But Randy could hear him, now.

Because Randy was his evil twin.

Randy came from a town where, if you couldn't tell whether someone was a man or a woman from one hundred yards away, you *had* to kick their ass. Randy was the closest thing to a fag, so they thumped him every chance they got, to try to stop him from going away, from rejecting them and following his dream.

He had come to Hollywood so full of hope, and he'd been passed down the food chain of vampires, lampreys and leeches, sucked dry and hollowed out until he was only the thinnest of shells around a howling void.

At last, he was the perfect actor.

"I know what this scene needs," he growled. The bathroom door sagged off its hinges when he slammed it and thundered across the hall to the back bedroom no bigger than the toilet and he ripped the closet door off its track and ripped up the floorboards and grabbed the mildewed duffel bag he knew would be there. He threw it over his shoulder like the boy it belonged to never could, and stomped back down the hall to enter the scene, stage left.

The audience shouted at him, the director leapt into his way, but Randy threw his hands out in a frustrated teenage gesture that clipped the director across the mouth and sent him sprawling into the crowd. Nobody else got in his way, because Randy disappeared. In his place, a skinny, pimply freckled kid stood with a duffel bag on his shoulder and a resolute stare burning a hole in the floor.

"Dad, we need to talk."

"Get off the stage!" a few in the crowd shouted, but others shut them up.

The big dyke in Dad's chair showed through for a second, but then she killed a beer and threw it into the crowd and the angry red-faced man stood up and said, "We're in the middle of an exercise, Tim." Dad looked around like he could see the words coming out of his mouth. "Scout has an audition tomorrow. If you want to come back and join the group—"

"No, I don't want to join the group." The kid dropped his duffel bag on the table. Something fell out of it. Moldy clothes and comic books and somebody in the crowd screamed because they saw something else. "I wanted to join a family, but you won't let us be one. I'm tired of living for *your* dream, Dad."

"Tim, sit down," Mother mumbled. She was busy underlining Trudy's lines for her commercial audition tomorrow.

"We'll talk about this later," Dad said. His eyes rolled in his head, trying to see the script, trying to figure out where his lines were coming from. No longer the star of the scene, he stared at this angry little live wire who came around the table to get in his face.

"Nobody here wants to be an actor, Dad. That was your dream…"

"And nobody handed it to me, I had to earn it! And I made it…How many situation comedies did you star in before you were ten? And my parents didn't…"

"They didn't push you like you push us! When your time ended, you moved out to the middle of nowhere and started a child star farm."

"Well, maybe I made a mistake, trying to help you, I admit that. Some people just don't have it. Kids, take note, your brother is trying to teach you something, in his own way. Giving up is pretty ugly, isn't it?"

Nobody said anything.

"We're not your puppets any more, Dad. I'm not an actor. I'm a human fucking being! I'm going to go out and find a regular loser job and marry a nobody wife and raise some nobody kids, and we're never going to be famous and we're never going to be rich, and we're going to go to bed at night happy."

"So GO! Don't let me stop you!" Dad came around the table and shoved him, but he had a steak knife in his other hand and when he shoved the kid into the wall, his hand whipped out with the knife. Randy felt it and he looked around but he couldn't see the crowd but he could feel them like a hundred-eyed invisible, loving God telling him, *No, don't give up!*

And he knows how the scene goes, the real scene ends with Tim dying at the hands of his failed child star Dad, but the crowd says NO, GET UP.

Randy caught his Dad's hand and pried it off the knife and socked Dad in the eye, sending him tumbling back into the table. Tim pulled the knife out of his side and raised it over his father, but then dropped it. He picked up his duffel bag and pushed his clothes back into it, and nobody could see the other thing, the tumble of black, moldy bones, now.

"Come with me! We can still be a family!"

Mother and his sisters looked down at the table, shrinking with shame as the spotlight contracted down to a pinpoint on him as he marched off the stage into the crowd. The family didn't stir, but the audience was swept up in it, they were all Tim when he crossed the room and threw open the front door and leapt off the porch that hung over the northbound lanes of the 101. One after another, they charged out the door after him, into the blinding lights and blaring horns and screeching tires of the world beyond broken dreams.

Cody Goodfellow has written four novels—*Radiant Dawn, Ravenous Dusk, Perfect Union* and *Repo Shark*—and co-wrote *Jake's Wake, Spore* and *The Last Goddam Hollywood Movie* with John Skipp. His short fiction has been collected in *All-Monster Action* and *Silent Weapons for Quiet Wars*, both of which received the Wonderland Book Award. As co-founder and editor of **Perilous Press**, he has presided over new Mythos releases by Brian Stableford, David Conyers and Michael Shea. He lives in Burbank.

Whisperings Sung Through the Neighborhood of Stilted Sorrows

by WC Roberts

1. Shadows

The wet nurse quit. Who could stand living
under that roof with hobgoblins climbing in
through the windows on moonless nights
and stealing down the hall
to whisper from behind closed bedroom doors,
trying to vaccinate the poor child
against schizophrenia? A hydra
with so many mouths to feed
and teeth like dirty needles...
they prick and set her breasts on fire

the shadow feeds, then
it sniffs at the breeze and rides on the night
to another broken soul beside the road
whirling beneath stars of Astor
and decay

2. Nativity

She goes out that door and down the road
with a carpet bag under her arm, its handle broken,
no longer wondering which way to go
but away—away, and awake. Not to sleep again.
A green flare goes up in the distance,
marking the changes in her
hour by hour as they go on adoring him,
his body in a knotty pine wood box.
Mourners of wax and bone
framed by rows of metal folding chairs,
their tears pooling on the floor in the parlor

swirls concentric and caressing
they have come
to sip angst from the delectable pool
and go on (unmoved and unaware)

3. Apprehension

A reliquary to be roasted,
this heart to be consumed. The organ does
what it was always supposed to do:
produce milk.
Everyone from the neighborhood comes
to suck, and find succor in her arms,
her gaping wounds.
They drip serum, nightly.

entering an open window, invisible on
the breeze it feasts upon
yet another darkened heart.
Nearly sated

4. Timewatching

He waits—as he always does—twitching
at each movement in the darkness,
the ticking of all his clocks
fails to sooth him.
He doesn't know if they'll come to him
but he believes they will,
seeking to drink from his veins—
veins throbbing, pulsing with liquid time.
He'll be ready when they come,
he thinks. Hopes. Dreaming

it rides to another pool of despair,
savoring the flavors of hopelessness
and resignation...
Going wherever the wind

5. Engravements

"T&R" marred the wood, deeply cut
into the trunk of the ancient oak at dusk
the orange bolding the engravement
as pitted, shadow letters off-centered
in this crudely drawn heart.
She was the "R" he remembers, but...
had he been the "T"? He comes to the oak

at the end of the day again and again
to see if the memory will return. It hasn't.
He wonders if the "X" carved into his temple
keeps the memories from coming back,
if someone told him it all before
and he just doesn't remember.
How could he? He

takes it, to dip in the sweetness
of night, resting in ancient oak leaves'
moist, black palimpsestuous layers
on the floor of the wood lot,
strangers locked up inside their houses
until the hunger again and again returns.

WC Roberts bought his first television in 2010, after selling his first 100 poems. He can't get Mystery Theater or Happy Days reruns on his rabbit ears, not way out where he is, so he Rarebit Dreams of riding in the sidecar with motorcycle-tough Miss Marple as she jumps the shark. Or tries to. Night after night. Desperate for a satellite dish, he applies his imagination to works of fiction.

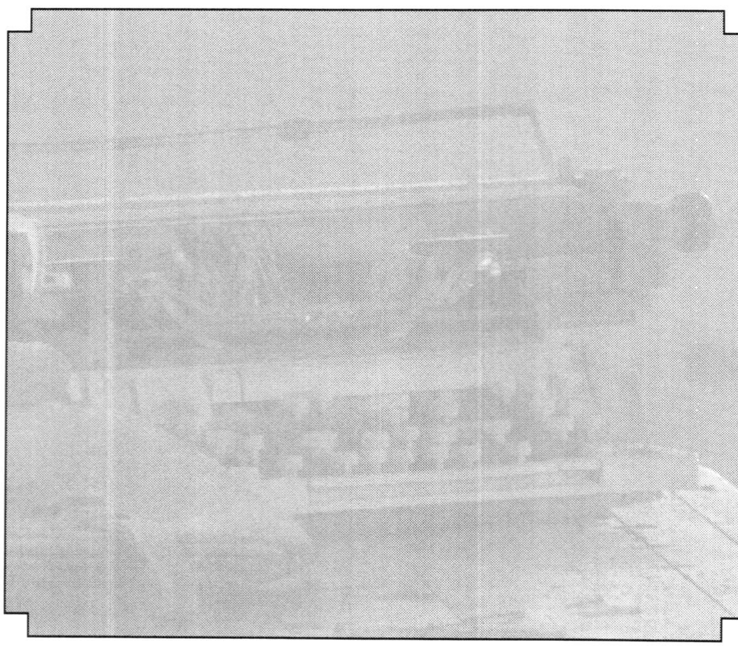

Strange Goods and Other Oddities

Books, Movies, Music and More

***Ex-Communication*, by Peter Clines; Broadway Books, 2013; 346 pgs.**

Ah, how much I love Peter Clines. His *Ex-* series has had me since the opening chapter of *Ex-Patriots*, when we were first introduced to the stable of new superheroes that populate his zombie-filled, post-apocalyptic vision of Los Angeles.

So much has changed since that first innovative book. The heroes' home, The Mount, has grown from a small compound where the survivors of the ex-virus struggle from day to day into a bustling city-within-a-city, complete with churches, marketplaces, and an actual police force. Legion, that offbeat master of the undead, still lingers outside their walls, trying occasionally to force his way inside and make life miserable for our heroes, but for the most part he's contained. His presence becomes a relative nuisance more than an actual threat, which is an interesting turn for this third novel to take. Whereas once Legion was the menace that seemed destined to bring about the final downfall of humanity as we know it, his existence has become simply another fact of life.

In the place of that baddest of baddies, the survivors of Los Angeles have seemingly mundane problems to deal with such as crime, religion, and political disagreement, all of which have been building for three books now. I thought it was brilliant to focus on these aspects of life within The Mount, as what is a new problem for the survivors is actually quite an old problem in the world that's now gone. It reads like the tail end of a loop before it whirls back around and starts on the cycle all over again. Is humanity doomed to repeat the failings of the past? Are ignorance, faith, and a fear of the unknown going to drive this new society into the same frenzied mess as the one that came before it? Will the heroes, who possess great abilities regular folk just can't aspire to, going to continue to be benevolent, or will they act upon their strength and become dictators rather than protectors? These are all powerful questions *Ex-Communication* asks, though since this is an ongoing series, they aren't answered just yet.

And into the midst of this, a new danger emerges, one that threatens to undo *everything*. In truth, this new threat—which encompasses the last third of the novel—is the weakest aspect of the story. Yes, it's tense and over-the-top and filled with action (as befitting any of the *Ex-* books), but there was something disappointing about it, as well. Maybe it's because the intriguing storyline of a certain character ends, one that I've been waiting to be resolved since the end of the first book, and that ending was less than satisfying.

Despite that, this last part of the story does tie into the feel of the rest of the book (not to mention the series as a whole). We finally get to meet Max Hale, a hero who is seen only as the reanimated demon Cairax in the first installment, and we see inside the mind of the powerful wizard and understand what makes him tick. And what is that, you ask? Ego, greed, ambition, selfishness, hubris. All the aspects of humanity that, in small doses, help to drive our race forward and yet, when applied to the extreme, threaten to destroy not just the individual, but all of those around them. In that way, Max represents all the new troubles brewing within their new city, which is a very, very clever maneuver by Clines. If only he'd come up a different way to bring about this end without sacrificing the most powerful and enigmatic of all the heroes in the process.

In all, this is a really fun read. Clines does some very interesting things with his mythology, including introducing a quirky undead girl whose mind regenerates each morning, wiping out her memory, which makes her the most innocent human of anyone in The Mount—aka a perfect counter to Max Hale's subterfuge. The book is filled with fantastic fight scenes and feats of super-powered fancy. Even including that one issue I had with the story, I think it's the best in the trilogy so far. A fresh perspective on zombie literature, which is a great thing since the genre has taken a definite turn for the dull worst. It's definitely on my short list of best books read in 2013, and it should be on yours too.

–Robert J. Duperre

Zombie Spaceship Wasteland, by Patton Oswalt; Simon & Schuster, 2011; 265 pgs.

I'm going to come out of the gate here and admit that I bent the parameters of the "horror" tie-in to review this book. I say that because aside from Oswalt's wonderfully nostalgic references to horror playing a part in his childhood and teenage years (both in film and literature), there is next to nil of the scary stuff in here. But that doesn't make it rock any less.

Zombie Spaceship Wasteland is a pseudo-memoir, all handed to us in that self-deprecating, sneaky snarky way that Oswalt has. His childhood and teen years in Virginia, working at a movie theater and playing Dungeons & Dragons, devouring volumes of fantasy and horror books—we start the ride there and go through to the early years of his comedy career. all peppered with hilarious anecdotes and darkly funny scenarios.

To break up the monotony, he throws in chapters of utterly strange things like "Chamomile Kitten Greeting Cards," all presented with little explanation, but they appear to be a line of greeting cards with ideas and historical rhetoric penned by Patton. Wryly hysterical to say the least.

The chapter on old Hobo songs

made me laugh so loud, my wife told me to put the book away as I was keeping her awake. There is a bittersweet chapter wherein his grandmother explains her increasingly bizarre gifts over the years.

The book is tied off with "Appendix A: Erik Blevins," which is an alter ego Oswalt created to pass time and break monotony when he was working in the script writing biz. Wild and off-kilter workups of ridiculous films that never were, such as *Cancer Pond*, *Slade Ripfire: Punch to Kill*, and what would be the best of the franchise, *Slade Ripfire: Deadly Blood-Kick to Oblivion*.

Not to snuff the flame he lights with "Appendix A," he delivers a second featuring the underground reviews of another persona, Neill Cumpston. We get to read his brutally honest and heartfelt reviews such as "Blade Fuckin' II, Fuck Yeah!" and "X2: X-Men Kicking You In the Balls So Hard That You Puke On Your Balls and Also Your Ass!" Just ridiculous.

I must admit, it probably helps if you're a fan of Oswalt's brand of humor, as this book reads like an extension of his routines. In fact, those familiar with his bits will no doubt recognize some constant themes as they show themselves in this book. But I found it quite fun and funny.

–John Boden

Apocalyptic Montessa and Nuclear Lulu: A Tale of Atomic Love, by Mercedes M. Yardley; Ragnarok Publications, 2013; 126 pgs.

When I read the title of the new novella by Mercedes M. Yardley, I itched to begin reading and find out what the two names meant and how the characters would find each other. "A tale of atomic love," the cover promised, and that drew me in ever further.

Having read Yardley's short story collection, *Beautiful Sorrows*, I thought *Apocalyptic Montessa* would be rich and sweet, like dense chocolate cake with a bitter, poisonous frosting. The opening was touching, a mother walking in a graveyard, naming her special child after a headstone that struck her—"Montessa." Then the unborn baby grew up, and became a stripper named Ruby.

You'd think that's where the sweetness stops, and to an extent, you'd be right. The beginning of this novella is heart-wrenching to read, although the pacing is so fast and engrossing that I had to force myself to put down my Kindle to do things like eat or sleep. Yardley's use of language and imagery is unparalleled, and *Apocalyptic Montessa and Nuclear Lulu* brings that in spades, as well as a rhythm to the prose that kept me enraptured.

The characters of Montessa and Lulu are lovely, broken demons that both drew me in and repelled me at times. It takes true skill to make characters that do such terrible things sympathetic, and I tip my hat to that deft hand. Just when I thought I couldn't take any more tension, the sweetness returns, and as a reader, I felt a bit guilty at the joy I felt for the two star-crossed lovers. Every second of that conflict is delicious.

–Catherine Grant

The Savage Dead, by Joe McKinney; Pinnacle, 2013; 368 pgs.

Did you ever read a book by a mainstream publisher and wonder how in the world that book ever got published? That was my thought as I read through Joe McKinney's failed attempt to bring a fresh perspective to the tired zombie genre.

Instead of focusing on the survivors of a world already gone to pot, or a core group just as the plague begins, McKinney decides to camouflage his zombie epic as a Clancyesque action-mystery tale of drug cartels and the men and women who fight against them, using the zombies only for the climax. This isn't necessarily a bad idea, and could have been a pioneering effort, but the author just couldn't pull it off.

The story revolves around Juan Perez, a superman undercover agent whose duty is to protect Senator Sutton, a woman who's pissed off the cartels with harsh legislation. Accompanying our perfect hero is Tess Compton, his super-sexy partner, and fighting against him is a cartel assassin named Pilar, also a super-sexy vixen who does her boss's bidding without question. Yes, everyone of importance in this book is a supermodel.

The first half of the novel is intrigue and deception as the good guys try to figure out which bad guys attempted to assassinate Senator Sutton. The bulk of the rest of the book takes place on a cruise liner, which Senator Sutton has decided to take to the coast of Mexico with only her husband, her assistant, and the super-sexy Tess Compton for protection. (Not exactly the best decision by a woman whose life is constantly in danger, but then again, if she hadn't made this decision, McKinney wouldn't have a book.) It seems one of the cartels has created a mutated flesh-eating bacteria that turns people into zombies, and it's super-sexy Pilar's job to release that virus on the cruise ship because…um…why not?

What follows is a muddle of events as Pilar takes over the ship, zombies run amuck, and Juan tries to figure out what's going on from the mainland. I've never read a book where the exciting bits were as trying as this one. The action seems hastily crammed together while the less interesting parts, such as the descriptions of weapons and the inner workings of a particular Secret Service detail, are long and tedious. McKinney obviously knows a ton about police work (he's a police officer himself), but for this book at least, he can't seem to rip himself away from the cop fantasy to tell an interesting story. It's strange.

The other large problem with *The Savage Dead* is the fact that it sees itself as a serious work of fiction, but is far too self-aware to have the emotional impact that such an offering would require. Sometimes it reads like a parody of itself, specifically in two instances: when Pilar interacts with her cartel bosses, and during the extended fallout of the zombie plague on the cruise liner. It's almost as if the author took stock characters, events, and motivations from the two separate genres and simply copied/pasted them onto the page. The only time the book seems truly original is when we're thrown into the past lives of the characters we're following. Their pasts are actually cohesive and even (in Pilar's case) intriguing. Yet the care displayed in crafting those back stories is thrown out the window once we return to the present. The characters become stock once more, almost as if they're pod people who still remember the events of the past but have no emotional connection to them. They simply do what they do to drive the story forward.

Anyway, enough piling on. Suffice to say that I didn't enjoy *The Savage Dead*. And I also don't think this particular book can be used to define McKinney as an author. His four-book *Dead World* series is beloved by his fans, so there has to be something there that folks love. But with this offering, let's just say it was a massive *fail*.

–Robert J. Duperre

Secret Things: 12 Tales to Terrify, by Stacey Longo; Books & Boos Press, 2013; 170 pgs.

You're flipping through the channels when you come across a horror movie. You see the TV schedule at the bottom of the screen shows that the movie is about to be over—and indeed, that is precisely when the bloody heroine creeps up behind the cocky villain, raises her knife, and STABS. Cut to black, roll credits.

Well, that ending sure got spoiled. With an annoyed sigh, you flip the channel.

A standup comedienne is on the next channel—and just then, she's delivering a raunchy punchline, and the audience—whom had gotten to hear the joke from the start—cracks the eff up.

Dammit! You're really missing out on some good treats. Can't you just catch a break and take in the whole *of a narrative, and not just the final note? The punchline, after all, is the dessert that's only sweet if you've already enjoyed the main course...*

At long last, there's a solution for this dilemma—a collection by Connecticut author (and co-owner of the great bookstore Books & Boos) Stacey Longo, called *Secret Things: 12 Tales to Terrify*. The stories contained herein deliver in full upon their promises of horror, featuring strong narratives, memorable characters, and at times downright *wicked* humor.

I'd be beating around the proverbial bush if I didn't come right out and say that I *loved* how they all ended. Have you ever read a story that seemed to meander aimlessly, and didn't end on a strong note? Well, that is never the case here—instead, Mrs. Longo ends each story with flair, often with biting humor and downright shocking twists. From the absolutely brilliant opening title story and on through several others such as "Denny's Dilemma" and "Trapped," Mrs. Longo has a knack for ending her stories with on jarring notes, often delivering their punchlines with casual, even matter-of-fact, flair.

The protagonists in these tales are richly illustrated and frequently very sympathetic, often paired off against extremely unlikeable people; I was flat-out *rooting* for some of the characters in their respective situations. I found myself identifying pretty deeply with some of the characters, too—their introverted thoughts were so familiar that at times I was wondering if I was projecting myself!

Among the standout tales is "Cliffhanger," which brings on the tension hard and fast from the get-go, as a woman falls from the edge of a cliff alongside the Grand Canyon, only to find herself perched on a narrow ledge between life and death. "Trapped" was a grim, claustrophobic, and unapologetic dark tale of a woman and her husband stuck in their house during a snowstorm. "Time to Let Go," of which I won't even divulge the details, was reminiscent of the works of Jackson, King, and Gaiman, as the plot slowly comes together, only to quietly pull the carpet out from beneath the reader at its conclusion.

There's even a piece of non-fiction found in the middle of it all—"Interlude: A Story That Failed" is a *secret thing* in its own right, and a good source of chuckles. (It's also a nice companion piece-*cum*-prelude to the story notes at the end of the book.)

Secret Things was more than a good escape; it was a darkly entertaining glimpse into the talented and delightfully twisted mind of a promising author. You won't want to miss out on what she does next—and how she'll end her next tale!

That evening, you don't even bother turning on the TV. You toss the TV remote to the wall, pick up your copy of Secret Things, *and start reading...*

–Barry Lee Dejasu

***The Best Horror of the Year: Volume Five*, Edited by Ellen Datlow; Night Shade Books, 2013; 406 pgs.**

Ellen Datlow's annual best-of anthologies are anticipated like prom. Getting even an honorable mention is akin to being on the news, a sure sign you're made some mark on the seemingly endless blackboard that is horror fiction. *Shock Totem* can proudly claim a few of our stories and authors have received mention in these volumes, in the past and in this one, volume five. The first chunk of pages are an enchilada of horror press name-checking, and then we get to the meat of the matter: the stories.

Lucy Taylor's "Nikishi" is a strong tale of retribution and demonic justice that sets us on our way, followed by Dan Chaon's "Little America," which is a freshly strange and deeply unsettling zombie story. A few stories later we are subject to "The Callers," by Ramsey Campbell, in which a young man is staying with his grandparents. Bored, he follows his Gran to the bingo hall—and from there things get very weird and weirder.

Gemma Files's "Nanny Grey" is a haunting tale of a haunted girl and the bad man who has unwholesome designs for her. Gary McMahon (one of my favorite authors; read his stuff!) turns in "Kill All Monsters," the tale of a man and his family held prisoner by his visions and the duties they bind him to. Paranormal investigators meet their match in "The House On Ashley Avenue," by Ian Rogers. Margo Lanagan's "Bajazzle" is a hypersexual and sinister tale about fidelity and lust. "The Pike," by Conrad Williams, is a wonderfully nostalgic tale of a man and an ugly fish. Very reminiscent of "Catfish Gods," by Weston Ochse.

Amber Sparks's "This Circus the World" may well be my favorite of the lot. Stunningly written and daring. Prose that reads very much like a poem, but the overall tone is so dark and lingering. Truly a beautiful piece of writing. Gary McMahon gets a second feature with "Some Pictures in An Album," where a young man clearing out his parents' estate comes across an album and the darkest of secrets he has hidden for too long. "Wild Acre," by Nathan Ballingrud, confronts guilt and terror and how that can suffocate a person when they join hands. Stephen Bacon's "None So Blind" is a grim scene story about a dying man and a blind woman. Adam G. Nevill gives us "Pig Thing," wherein a family is attacked by the titular creature, though very little of the terror comes from the monster.

All of the stories contained in this collection are good. I have mainly singled out the ones that stuck with me. Datlow is known for her discerning tastes in short fiction and she has once again proven that to be true. A very eclectic and entertaining omnibus of short fiction that some folks may have missed out on last year. Remedy that.

–John Boden

Cain's Blood, by Geoffrey Gerard; Touchstone, 2013; 353 pgs.

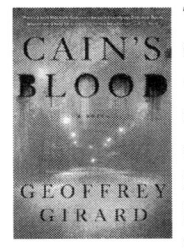

The premise of Geoffrey Gerard's debut novel, *Cain's Blood*, is enough to make any horror aficionado pluck it from the shelf and give it a good once over. Clones of the world's most infamous serial killers have escaped from a government-funded facility, leaving a trail of violent crimes in their wake. Shawn Castillo, a former black ops soldier, has been tasked with the capture of the escaped clones and ultimately teams up a young boy created from the genes of Jeffery Dahmer. What's not to love?

Sadly, the brilliance of the premise is tarnished by the delivery. This is largely due to the novel's rapid pace. Reading *Cain's Blood* is akin to traversing a carnival in a rocket car. There are plenty of cool things to see, but most of the time you're moving far too fast to get a good look. Much of the plot has the characters moving from state to state in pursuit, but little of the scenery is ever mentioned. Likewise, many of the houses and hotel rooms are cycled through with little attention to detail. What's worse is that this breakneck speed kills much of the suspense the novel could have had. In the horror genre, pacing is King. No amount of crime scenes or gallons of blood can change that. At its heart, *Cain's Blood* is more of a thriller one might take to the beach than a horror novel.

In terms of characterization, those who populate the novel often fall into worn tropes, particularly the protagonists. The damaged soldier seeking redemption and the misunderstood youth can feel paper thin in places, and the reader isn't given solid reasons to cheer them on until later in the book. Additionally, the young clone is clearly used as a poster child for the nature vs. nurture debate, turning him into more of a medium for the author's thoughts on the subject than a fully-realized character. The escaped killers themselves also leave something to be desired in terms of development as much of their characterization is heavily dependent on the personas of the originals to the point of it being a crutch, overshadowing any personal experience the clones might have, at least in the case of those partaking in the killing spree.

One of the stronger aspects of the novel is the information on cloning sprinkled throughout. Girard has done his homework, and it certainly shows. From a brief overview of cloning to open the novel to lectures on various government experiments and cover-ups, plenty of ground is covered. While this can sometimes turn into a heavy-handed info dump as a character proceeds to tell the reader about a dozen related events at a go, these insights tend to be some of the more enjoyable sections the book has to offer.

While the use of facts regarding real events makes progress toward cementing the premise in reality and making it more believable, almost every plot choice in the novel works to do the exact opposite. Between the addition of other government science experiments and Hollywood style shootouts, much of the novel ends up coming off as outlandish rather than convincing. Throw in a number of gaps in logic regarding the behavior of the escaped clones and a highly convenient ending and everything becomes a little too unstable. The suggestion that a clone of John Wayne Gacy would be genetically predisposed to wearing a clown suit and makeup is tenuous at best, as is the concept that a handful of homicidal loners would pile in a car for a murderous road trip.

It may be worth pointing out that the Internet is full of praise for the novel, and that while reading these reviews I felt as though I had experienced something entirely different from the average reviewer. If you're looking to read something that is quick and requires little mental effort to digest, *Cain's Blood* may be for you. However, if you are looking for something with prose that goes the extra mile and suspense served up with a good, old-fashioned sense of dread, it may be best to look elsewhere.

–Zachary C. Parker

Interested in having your material
reviewed in an upcoming issue of
Shock Totem
or on our website?

Please e-mail us at
reviews@shocktotem.com

Watchtower

by D.A. D'Amico

Just before dawn. The mosquitos had given up trying to feast on dying men. Air, boiling steam during the day, had congealed to a thick sultry fog that clung to the brush like tar. Sour earthy odors from the jungle mixed with the raw stench of unwashed bodies as I cupped my hand over Dex's mouth.

He gasped once and sagged back, the fight draining out of him. None of us had much struggle left. It had been beaten out, worn away until lying down to die was the easiest thing. But capture didn't mean surrender, not to me.

"Shut it!" I yanked the little bundle of manioc paste from Dex's hands. It was as much as I dared stash from the VC, and it would have to get us as far as Dong Ha—if the Marines still held that base, and if the North Vietnamese hadn't overrun the DMZ. "Don't make me go alone."

Dex blinked his big crazy eyes and nodded. He'd been singing again, humming that gritty whisper he said was "her" song and pursing his lips like a fish on asphalt. I thought the jungle had gotten to him, or the beatings, but others had seen her too.

"She's calling." He shook me off, staggering up a small mound of stone tailings in the direction of the silo, tugging on the stump of his mangled left leg. The moon cast jagged shadows over the little hill, serrated lines of pale silver light that made the thick jungle appear black. I shouldn't have brought him. I knew he'd bug on me, but Marines stick together. Semper Fidelis.

I slid down, small stones clattering as they cascaded under my bare feet. I crouched. Our prison wasn't bars or towers, but the Viet Cong still patrolled the tight cluster of huts as if the heavy brush were made of barbed wire.

"Go, get away." Dex had already found the worn dirt trail we used every day to shuffle from our prison shack to the tiny quarry. "She needs me."

I grabbed him. In the dark, his eyes looked otherworldly, huge black-rimmed mirrors that reflected pieces of the waning moon. I shook with the effort not to punch him, trying to remember that Charlie had messed him up. He'd taken twenty hard lashes with a rattan cane and three days in the tiger pit for his first escape attempt. They'd cut his left foot off on his second, hacked through it with the same machetes they used to trim the bamboo struts. They'd kill him if they caught him this time, and me along with him.

We didn't have time for hallucinations.

"Don't do this. We all see things in our dreams. Hell, I've even seen your girl." He stopped struggling. "You?"

Two nights ago, I'd dreamed of the waifish beauty that had appeared in the thoughts of at least five men. She came to me with an eerie song on her full lips, her lean features giving her an elfish quality. The scent of apple blossoms shimmered around her like heat, making it impossible to glance away from her big green eyes. I'd been scared enough not to return to sleep. She'd gotten inside my head.

I'd heard her again earlier tonight, calling just after lights out, and decided then that it was time. Our escape couldn't wait any longer. The jungle, with its rotting stench, incessant rainfall, and brutal heat, was winning.

"It's only wishful thinking," I said.

"She's more, much more. You'll see." His tone spooked me, as if he'd been brainwashed. Charlie had done more than just ruin his body; they'd messed up his head, and I didn't want to wait around until they did the same to me.

When I'd first suggested escape, Dex had been all over it. He had a girl in Osaka, someone special, and it was worth his life to get back to her. He could talk about nothing else. Now, he only had thoughts for his dream woman. Me, I had the Corps, and an old man stateside to whom I needed to prove a thing or two, so I was running no matter what.

~

"Dex, this is it. Turn around." We crested the small trail. I hadn't realized how close we'd gotten to the small area we'd liberated from the jungle in order to reveal that enigmatic ring of stones.

"Wait!" I heard talking in the distance, curt Vietnamese words shot back and forth like rifle fire. I pulled Dex to the ground, my breath rapid, and my limbs tingling. "They're up to something."

Through the trees, I could see the outline of the thing we called the silo. Some trick of the moonlight made it seem enormous, like a long-abandoned medieval keep. It reminded me of pictures my dad had shown me of the castles he'd visited during his tour in the last good war. The memories felt like déjà vu. Those strongholds had been burned-out piles of rock stretching like fists into the sky, and each one reeking of mystery. I thought I'd like to visit them someday, but here in the jungle south of Da Nang, trapped behind enemy lines, beaten and forced to hump rocks, I'd lost the child inside of me.

The Marines recruited me in sixty-seven because my old man was a jarhead, and his old man before him. I got shipped in-country in sixty-eight, and it was only a short while before I found myself on the wrong side of action, out of ammo and trapped under a heap of my dead and dying buddies.

Charlie had rounded up two dozen of us and marched us out to the middle of nowhere, double-time, with three dead from exhaustion before they'd finally let up. We thought we were in hell, but that was before they'd forced us to pull boulders out of the soupy black earth with wooden shovels, day after sweltering day, week after festering week.

"What are they saying?" I asked. Dex knew a bit of Vietnamese, picked it up during his time in Saigon. It all sounded like quacking to me.

The light shifted. The tower stood out among the palmyra and ebony trees as if lit from within, a cool blue radiance covering the outer stones like a sheath.

"They're talking about the stones," Dex whispered. "Trying to figure out if it needs to be higher. They're not sure."

There'd been a circle about fifty feet around when we'd arrived, vine choked and lichen crusted, a scattering of stones no higher than my shoulder. We'd put forty feet of blood into the height of it, suffering in the heat and the mosquitos to raise boulder after boulder along the bamboo framework while the grim VC soldiers paced back and forth below.

He turned. His smile looked like an uneven row of pebbles in his mouth. "She calls, can you hear her?"

A soft moaning gurgled from the structure, like wind whistling through notches in the bamboo. It made the skin on my neck tickle. Interspaced, I caught snatches of song, but not ghostly elfin music, something more familiar. Jimi Hendrix's deep buttery voice throwing out some Bob Dylan lyrics, a hit from last year's *Electric Ladyland* album.

"They're all here." Dex's voice came out in a drool, words spilling over each other in a hurry. "They're working already, hoisting the last stone in position. Come on, or we'll miss it."

He started hobbling, the stump of his left foot clomping in the hard-packed earth.

"What about the escape?" The words fell lame from my lips.

~

Three Viet Cong soldiers stood beside the ramp. Dark narrow eyes and squat expressionless features traveled along the high wall. Purple spots arced through my retinas, and I tensed. I thought I heard a woman laughing.

"They can't hear her. This was supposed to be something big, something magical, and they can't feel it." Dex laughed. He winked at me as if we shared a private joke, and then he mumbled something in Vietnamese

~

We waited until the VC marched from sight, and then I picked up Dex and shuffled over to the bamboo framework. I couldn't believe I was doing this, but something about the music pulled me forward.

"I don't understand." I helped my friend get a footing on the rough plank ladder.

I shook my head, still too dazed to think straight. My movements felt mechanical, as if I stood outside my body while someone else controlled my actions. He scrambled up the casing ropes like a monkey, heading for the top. The music got louder. Hendrix's guitar echoed over granite that seemed to glow brighter with each note. I followed him, passing teams of American soldiers. These were men who'd been too beaten down to lift themselves off their makeshift beds, but who were now singing and hauling rocks that flamed in their hands like napalm. Their grim faces shone with the same intensity as the stone.

The top surged with emerald fire, arcs of jade passing through the immense glowing circle. A thin fog rose from within the well created by the ring of boulders. Dex teetered at the edge, glancing through the gap as if staring across a vast forest. His lips moved. I couldn't hear his words over the music, but I could see the way his expression changed. He spoke to her.

The hair at the back of my neck bristled. I felt a longing sadness, an ache to see deeper. Something wondrous and terrible waited beyond my vision. He could see it, but it eluded me like the hope of escape.

I took a step back, and at the same moment Dex took a leap forward.

"No!"

He spread his arms, not to fly, but in welcome. Then he slid out of sight. I fell to my knees, stunned. Dex was the closest thing to a brother I'd ever had.

The music got louder. It throbbed through my brain, disrupting my concentration, messing with my thoughts. Charlie had tortured me with acoustics during my first weeks in. Those memories burst over me like fireworks, and I screamed.

"She calls." The frail-looking infantry grunt with the dark Fu Manchu moustache and blunt sagging nose pushed by, falling into the bright haze. I watched him until he reached the bottom, but didn't see him hit.

Hunt and Bouchard, the two New Englanders who'd confessed to seeing the fantasy woman in their dreams went next, stepping into the gap as if marching at parade.

The music overwhelmed me, screeching notes that had lost all semblances of tone and balance. I held my ears and cried as soldiers plunged into the pit, some leaping, others casually striding, and a few who got a running start. I spun, searching for the radio. If I could stop that, then maybe I could put an end to all of this. I couldn't think.

Charlie had done something to our heads. Maybe they were experimenting with drugs, or maybe I sat rotting in the tiger pit, and this was nothing but a nightmare.

~

The music stopped abruptly. Hendrix vanished in a purple haze, and I was left alone.

The ringing in my ears turned to a soft shushing, like the ocean, or a faint lullaby. The cold fire in the stones subsided, and thin tendrils of fog slunk down the seams of rock and back into the earth below. The tingling sense of wonder returned with an echo of a long forgotten greatness that left me hollow and empty inside, as if I'd missed something miraculous.

I felt her presence, the scent of her like a coating on my tongue. She was still out there, still within the circle we had made for her in this world, waiting. Tears poured down my cheeks. I stepped to the edge, but could see no path. My road wasn't paved with faith as theirs had been, and I could see no easy escape.

I stepped from the tower anyway.

D.A. D'Amico is a playful soul trapped in the body of a grumpy old man. In early years, this presented a problem, but David has been growing into the role quite nicely. He's had nearly two dozen works published in the last few years, and can be found at www.dadamico.com.

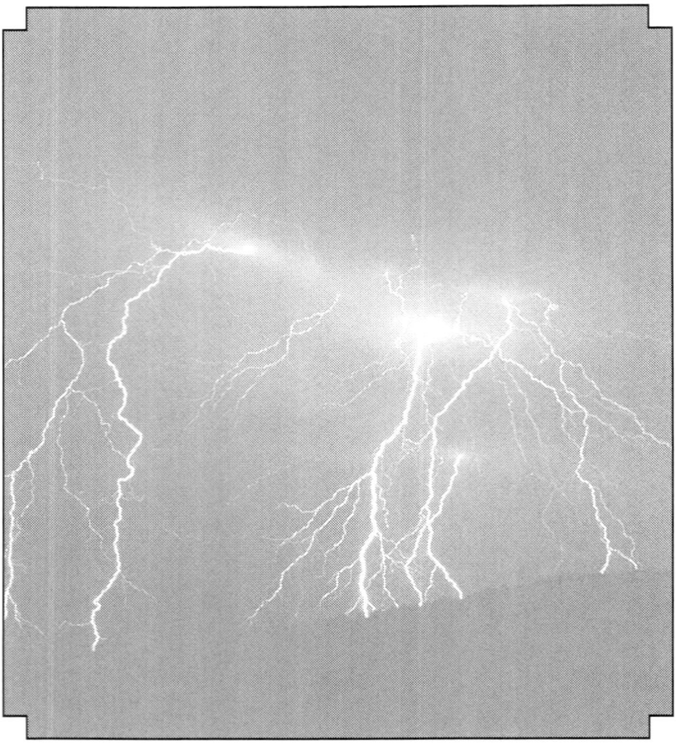

Death and the Maiden

by David Barber

1

Pitchforks and torches. This mob howls like the one that harried Frankenstein. Now I know the perils of acquiring knowledge, and how much happier is the man who believes his native town to be the world.

This rabble, my neighbours, my own relatives perhaps, have discovered my secret toil in the unwholesome damps of the grave and will not forgive me for it.

2

These are my parents. I am their only child. Look at the expression on their faces. No offspring should carry the burden of so much ignorant hope. There was another child, stillborn I think, but they never mention it. Perhaps they comfort themselves knowing they gave everything for me and could not have sacrificed more. And now I am suddenly home, without a position or degree. My parents know nothing of science. They think I would be paid for publishing papers and can imagine no other reason for doing so.

"Dr Frankenstein has gone to the Arctic you say?"

"Pursuing his research."

My father looks puzzled. "We heard…"

What have they heard? More slanders and lies about a visionary? They understand nothing.

My mother hurries to interrupt, as she always does, to appease any unpleasantness. "Then this is a holiday for you. You deserve a rest."

"I intend to continue Dr Frankenstein's work."

3

I have ordered the crates from Frankenstein's laboratory to be delivered to the cottage. This ramshackle dwelling in the forest is my mother's meagre inheritance.

Dr Frankenstein was a great man, not bound by petty rules; he discovered more in a few years than an age of cautious minds, yet he was also careless of everything but his work. He never asked where his anatomical samples came from. It was I who sought out equipment and chemicals, and I who spent his money as carefully as if it was my own. I still have coin enough for months.

Still, I see no reason to repeat his mistakes. Why did he need to assemble bodies? Why the obsession with electricity? Did he not see the key to unlocking the secrets of life was to be found in life itself?

We shall see whose name is in the history books.

4

We are so proud of you, my parents say. They have invited guests to a dinner party. Perhaps things have changed, for I do not remember them ever entertaining like this. Then I realise it is in my honour, like someone famous returning to the place of their birth. And because of their inexperience, or because they know so few people, it is an awkward and bourgeois gathering. I know only my aunt and uncle, who run a shoe factory. They bring their daughter-in-law, Katya, already a young widow it seems.

While I was away, my cousin managed to marry, father a child and die of septicaemia. Others acquire lives so effortlessly, plunging into the current, while I paddle at the water's edge.

I am not at ease with women, and I wait for the look on her face as she observes the scoliosis of my spine, but her expression reveals nothing but the bruising of fatigue around her eyes.

"You study natural philosophy, I hear."

Her dark hair positively gleams. It is parted in the middle and caught up behind by some contrivance, leaving her neck exposed. A slender, bared neck. I know these pert ambitious sort of women, they have discounted me on many occasions, but loss and worry seem to have softened this one.

"He works for Dr Frankenstein of Geneva," says my father. "A distinguished family,"

"Works with Dr Frankenstein," corrects my mother. I always implied we were colleagues, and the matter is too far gone now to correct.

"Franz was a surgeon," Katya says. "But of course you knew that, you grew up together."

Oh yes, and was always his lackey in our dealings, and later his whipping boy. It is one of the shames of my youth that I did not cast off his thrall sooner. My mother has already explained how he nicked himself amputating a gangrenous foot and succumbed to the infected cut. My indifference seemed to shock her.

In Katya's mind, science and medicine are twins, so she tells me about her son and the fits he suffers. This is her first social outing since the death of her husband, and she confides her guilt at leaving her boy with others tonight.

Earlier, as I tried to read, my mother described the woes of this sickly child, wracked by epilepsy. She lowered her voice as she spoke of a husband untimely taken, and now perhaps a son. She spends pity like pennies.

"Doctors," Katya says helplessly, her dark eyes gleaming in the candlelight.

5

Later I find myself amongst the men, few of whom knew me, or one another.

"Ygor," confides my uncle. "Listen to this."

My uncle has found a congenial companion, some sort of transport agent used by my father, the man clearly surprised to find himself invited. He accepts a cigar from the box my father keeps for Christmas, and tucks it away in his top pocket. He winks at me.

"Jurgen here says there has been a desecration. A fresh grave opened. The authorities are keeping it quiet."

The transport agent explains. "In the Jewish cemetery you know. But still, it shows no respect for the dead. The body was not stolen, you understand, so not resurrection-men."

Casually, I ask if anything was done to the body.

"It could be the churchyard next," adds my uncle.

6

I confirm to Katya what everyone knows, that there is no cure for epilepsy, but hint at better ways to ease the suffering after an attack. While I casually mention the prestigious medical school where Dr Frankenstein studied, I think of his medical books. They will tell me more than any country doctor knows of palliatives for grand mal.

These are exciting times, I explain. Science is discovering new medicines, novel ideas about microbes. Does she know about microbes?

An infection that kills its host dooms the microbes also. It must be advantageous to the microbe to be less harmful, even to cause no damage at all. Countless millions of such harmless microbes probably live in each of us. But what if we pursued the idea further, what of microbes that prolong the life of their host?

It is foolish to reveal so much, but what else have I to impress her with but my cleverness?

7

Problems, nothing but problems. Small mammals do not live long after reanimation. They fade again after a few hours and a second dose of the microbe serum is ineffective. It may be the body fights the very microbes that preserve it. The lifespan of bigger animals should be greater. I have hopes that a human might survive much longer. It is not a universal panacea for death then. But surely, to reclaim someone, a child, for a day, even for an hour, is to be on the side of life.

I have invited her to the cottage, with the potions her doctors have prescribed. She may bring the boy if she wishes. This is where it begins, like something rising from the depths. If you have a thought you cannot unthink it.

8

Fretfully, she paces up and down. Her son is convalescing after an attack this very morning; they grow more frequent it seems. He is sleeping off the nausea and the headache in a darkened room. She fears her child worsens and the doctors do nothing. Now I am the focus of her helpless hopes.

Covertly I study her, fascinated by her long fingers as she wrings her hands, by the way her slender wrists make her dress look too short in the sleeve. She proffers the pills and medicines I asked for. It is laudanum mainly, and cream of tartar, lavender. Useless. Worse than useless. She is waiting for me to speak and I see how much of doctoring is an air of confidence.

"There are better treatments," I say, handing her the drug I have prepared. "Follow the instructions on the bottle carefully."

Even in daylight her face is pale. "How do I know it is safe?"

Safe? Her son has an incurable illness that is commonly fatal. And he is treated by doctors who have addicted him to opium.

"I have something important to show you."

"I must be home before my son wakes."

"Here," I insist, lifting the sheet from the cat.

There is something about the limpness of a dead animal that convinces without listening for a heartbeat. The head dangles as I lift the animal to pierce the carotid artery, repeatedly drawing the ground-glass barrel of the syringe in and out. The blood is still warm.

She turns away in disgust. "Why are you showing me this?"

How can I explain? I do not have the skills of Frankenstein. I cannot sew together the parts of men, knitting together vessels and nerves, ready for the shock of their animation. But I have come to believe the vital force was not just electricity, but certain microbes in the very corpses he worked with, in fluids extracted from the recently interred. I cannot bring matter to life as Frankenstein did, but death is not beyond my reach.

This I do tell her: Though there is much to be learned, it is not past conjecture that one day people will thank me for bringing back their loved ones, their children, themselves.

Katya stifles a scream and points. The cat arches its back and spits, then jumps off the table and is gone.

9

It is the kind of night Frankenstein would have wished for: Lightning over the forest to the south, the dull complaint of thunder, rain drumming on the roof. My latest experiment confirms that the survival of dogs is proportional to their size. Distressed, they wander the cottage, barking at shadows and empty corners. This one forces its head beneath my hand, whimpering, needing to be stroked. Yet I will have to bury even the Dane by morning.

Outside, I catch the sound of a carriage, stopping, then departing again. Cautiously I open the door onto the thrashing blackness of trees, and Katya steps into the light. Before I can ask what she is doing here, she brushes past me.

She opens her cloak. Such a small bundle in her arms. There is something about the limpness of a dead child that convinces without listening for a heartbeat.

"This morning," she says in a tiny voice. "During a fit. They do not know I am here."

It is the mystery of death. If you have sat by the dying and watched, you will understand the unreasonableness of that moment. A living person has gone, how can this be?

"I know it is wrong, but he was unjustly taken. Bring him back to me."

10

I have skills, I was as clever as any of them. What did my accent and clothes matter? But they were the sons of gentlemen, careless and confident, polishing off their educations. In practical matters I was even their superior, and the professors praised my work, yet I caught the amusement in the looks of my peers.

I shivered in a room above a wash-house in Ingolstadt, living on penny bread, trying to make sense of books in Latin, unable to tell my parents the money they scrimped together was never enough, that students of science must buy equipment too, and books, and materials, must know more than I learned in a country school.

Often I wake sweating from the dream of my disgrace, not even able to understand the questions. You must wait for the exam to end, they insist, but I run from the hall, from the eyes of everyone.

I continued to send letters home, blotted with lies. I do not know how it would have ended had Viktor Frankenstein not stopped me in the street. He had missed me in chemistry classes recently and wished to ask a favour.

I remember it clearly. "Perhaps we should go for a drink," he said. "Isn't that what students do?"

Of course it would mean I could not afford to eat that day. He clapped me on the shoulder, the raised shoulder no one mentions. It was as if I had spoken my thoughts aloud. "Or if you are busy, shall we just chat as we walk?"

University was all very well for those who played at learning, he declared, his look including me in those for whom it was not a game. He had his own ideas, and knew my skills in the laboratory...

"Mama," says the child, and reaches up a hand to her face.

11

Now, of course, you know how it ends.

She stays here with me, with her son, though it is not as I imagined. She will do anything to preserve the life of her child, though I see now that I disgust her. I have tried to explain the problem with the microbe serum, but she will not listen, and there is nothing I can say that does not make me sound like a vengeful God. We live in a kind of dark Eden, never speaking of the future, not acknowledging death.

"I had a strange dream, mama," the child says, but is too young to explain.

I thought the lad would grow bored and want to be out playing, but he seems fearful of the forest and clings to his mother instead, never smiling, always in the way.

"What does that man want with you?" he pipes, stroking his mother's hair and staring at me, his gaze somehow too frank and knowing.

"I do not like the way he looks at you, mama."

I should be making notes, recording this experiment, but the pages remain blank. For the first time, I find myself troubled by religious questions. What dreams disturbed Lazarus, woken back to life from Eternity? And did he resent the hand that returned him? I ask because there is something unwholesome about the child.

I have watched him fondle his mother's breast as she sleeps. He sees me and I cannot match his gaze.

12

"Inject him again," she screams. She will not listen, and her eyes burn with febrile brightness.

I have debated with myself how to proceed. If I take her back to town (if she will go, if she even allows me to touch her now) there would be questions. Her distress has gone beyond hysteria; she believes I made promises and broke them.

Perhaps a tiny grave in the forest, I hint. With flowers. She does not even answer.

The world would condemn me, but I feel no guilt, nothing of the pettiness of right and wrong. I have simply gone further than other men towards the far edge of things. The drug was mainly laudanum, but with something to weaken the child's heart. Enough so the strain of a fit would be too much. Was it not doomed anyway?

Perhaps I might spin a convincing tale if there were two graves deep in the forest. And no flowers to mark them. How long would an adult live after the microbe treatment? A question amenable to experiment. But of course, there was the hired carriage that brought her that night. Eventually they will think to look for her here. The fatal truth leaks out like water through cupped hands.

We fashioned monsters, Frankenstein and I, though mine has taken a lifetime to create.

David Barber lives anonymously in the UK. He used to be a scientist, though he is retired now and writing stories. He is a puzzle to his friends.

Bloodstains & Blue Suede Shoes

by John Boden and Simon Marshall-Jones

PART VI: THE MID TO LATE SEVENTIES

As the 70s were approaching their middle age, the music was mutating faster than ever. The saccharine sentiments of the hippie generation—peace, flowers in your hair, and free love—were being painted over in black. Those ideals were being stomped flat by an invasion from the UK, with bands of the caliber of Black Sabbath and Led Zeppelin. Creativity and genres were cross-pollinating, creating vicious, menacing hybrids while pop and rock were sprouting other heads, with thicker and sharper teeth. Hawkwind were delivering sci-fi-laced space rock and Genesis were still getting darkly proggy. Another British band, Deep Purple, were gaining not only considerable hard rock holding power but also legions of hardcore fans. Those bands and others of their ilk were the origins of the future of rock and roll, dark reflections shaded in heavy metal and hard rock, punk rock, and even disco. By the end of this decade the playing field would never be the same.

I SWEAR I SAW YOUR FACE CHANGE...
IT DIDN'T SEEM QUITE RIGHT

The year 1972 saw the debut album from Blue Öyster Cult, a band which would soldier on with a tenacity that would ultimately gain them an enormous cult following, if not mainstream popularity. Starting out as Soft White Underbelly in 1967 (then Oaxaca, followed by The Stalk-Forrest Group), in 1971 the band took the name under which they'd become rock superstars from a line in a poem written by their manager, Sandy Pearlman. The "Blue Oyster Cult," according to the poem, was a group of aliens who had gathered to secretly guide Earth's history. The band's music and album artwork were peppered with occult images and themes as well as dark science fiction and alchemy. Over their decades-long career, they would record and release many sinister anthems, from the hits "Don't Fear the Reaper" and "Godzilla" to the equally chilling later tunes like "Joan Crawford." Later albums featured songs with lyrics written by one of the originators of splatterpunk, author John Shirley. Blue Öyster Cult still tour occasionally.

During this same period of time and just under rock's radar, the band Elf, featuring a young Ronnie Dio on bass and vocals, was turning out killer blues rock. Only after taking jobs fronting the bands Rainbow and Black Sabbath in the 1980s would Dio, by then known as Ronnie James Dio, achieve the high level of fame and respect due him. By the time of his death from stomach cancer in 2010, Dio had become synonymous with the term "heavy metal."

Another of the more criminally overlooked rock bands from this time was the band Lucifer's Friend, coming off like the unholy stepson of Deep Purple and

Black Sabbath. They dropped their self-titled debut in 1970 and kept churning out records (though never again as dark and heavy as the debut) until they disbanded in 1982. They later regrouped as Lucifer's Friend II and released one album, 1994's *Sumo Grip*, before disbanding again a few years later.

In 1974, a band from New York City—one which would forever change the way the game was played in regard to marketing and promotion—would release their debut album. This band called themselves Kiss.

"Being a child of the 70s, I (John) was intrigued by these guys—I thought them a bizarro mix of comic book supervillains and space aliens. The makeup and fire-breathing theatrics and...hell, Gene Simmons was supposed to have had his tongue surgically forked. How fucking wild is that? I recall a babysitter when I was a kid—I'm going to guess maybe 1976 or early '77—she came to the house to watch us kids one evening and she brought some albums by Kiss and Ted Nugent. I don't think I ever recovered."

Kiss were everywhere. They had lunchboxes, Halloween costumes, comic books (with the band members' blood in the ink!), and in 1977 they delivered one of the worst of the so-bad-it's-cool gifts any band ever gave their fans: a made-for-TV movie called *Kiss Meets the Phantom of the Park*. Kiss are still around, albeit with only two original members, and still release albums with some regularity. They can still out-promote and shill anyone, and that must account for something.

While Kiss was forcing the leather glove of glammy shock rock down America's teen throats, we had Aerosmith revamping smut-rock blues and taking it to the streets. We also had the seminal New York Dolls preening and pouting with vicious glam abandon and singing about "Frankenstein" and "Trash." Iggy and his Stooges were bringing the noise and a raw ferocity that was inspiring masses. An inspiration that would be felt for decades. While the fires of expression were very much burning bright, there was nevertheless a sense that the rock dinosaurs of the early 70s were becoming irrelevant, and that the youth of the day were searching for something new and exciting, yearning perhaps for a musical experience that would come close to how it must have felt for the teenagers of the 50s and 60s, when popular music was fresh and vital, alive even.

It would be no exaggeration to say that musical culture was divided between the light and frothy "pop" scene, and the esoteric and bloated "rock" scene, where music was more often than not perceived as self-indulgent. Indeed, that yearning was felt on both sides of the Atlantic—and before long, the seismic rumblings of the earthquake of change were being felt.

I GOT A FEELING INSIDE OF ME... IT'S KIND OF STRANGE, LIKE A STORMY SEA

In the UK, punk emerged from the pubs and clubs of London and other places in the mid-70s, with bands like the Sex Pistols, The Damned, The Soft Boys, The Clash, 999, The Vibrators, and Siouxsie & the Banshees. In terms of "horror," only the Damned have come close to utilizing such imagery, and then only much later than the period we're currently dealing with. (Needless to say, we'll be covering them in a later installment of this series.) It is also a truism that British punk tended to deal with different themes than those of their cousins across the water—mainly street culture, social awareness, and the vacuity of establishment conservatism and conformity. Rebellion was the keyword here. Although it had not yet been christened with a name, the early grindings of Industrial music were poking their pale heads from beneath darkened stones. From the blippy electro-pop of bands such as Kraftwerk to the punk-turned-gothic Gary Numan, with or without his Tubeway Army, to the extremely dark nightmare fuel of Throbbing Gristle. The boundaries stretched, and in places, disappeared altogether. The curtains were torn and set aflame.

Across the pond, though, it was around this same time that the legendary New York club CBGBs started showcasing bands that would later be identified with the new wave and punk scenes. The club itself opened its doors in 1973, originally to put on bands closely allied to the actual name of the club—Country, BlueGrass, and Blues—but somehow in just three years it left those traditional genres behind and began promoting the likes of The Ramones, Blondie, Television, The Voidoids, The Fleshtones, and Talking Heads. Punk and new wave were set fair to revamp the entire face of music, giving rise to the independent scene we take so much for granted today. No longer did we have the side-long musical and lyrical extravaganzas of the prog-rock and stadium rock eras. Instead, we got short, sharp three-minute stabs of angst and energy, virulently anti-corporate iconoclasm, smashing down the barriers of the rarified musical spheres with joyful abandon and glee. Lyrical content was much nearer the earthly and gritty, very much the antithesis of just about everything which had gone before—in other words, it was much more relevant and immediate, socially and philosophically. If youth had been yearning for something which represented them, they'd definitely found it.

Among the graduates of CBGBs were The Cramps and The Misfits, both of whom had a close relationship with the darker side both musically and lyrically. The Cramps formed in 1976 by the husband and wife duo of Lux Interior and Poison Ivy, and remained active until the untimely death of Lux in 2009. Their take was on the trashier facet of the horror genre, particularly on the grindhouse and B-movie sectors. Song such as "I Was a Teenage Werewolf" and "Zombie Dance" off their debut album, *Songs the Lord Taught Us*, announced their chosen *oeuvre* in blood-red letters. Their sound was primal and stripped-back, striking chords with the primitive heart of fans and listeners, a rich vein the band continued to mine with success over the course of a further seven studio albums.

The Misfits, led by frontman Glenn Danzig, went even deeper into the horror genre, practically inventing the subgenre of horror punk in the process. Dark themes abounded, particularly in their second studio album, *12 Hits from Hell*, in which they set out their philosophical and cultural stall with song titles such as

"Halloween," "Vampira," "Night of the Living Dead," "Horror Hotel," and "Astro Zombies." Without wanting to overstate the case, The Misfits were a highly influential band, inspiring much later outfits to emulate both music and their onstage look (stark black and white facepaint, psychobilly hairstyles, and leather clothing). It would be fair to say that, without them, the goth and extreme metal scenes would never have happened in the way they did.

The explosion of the punk and new wave scenes gave an impetus and energy which managed to revive the moribund and ultimately superficial music industry of the day. It kicked it into high gear, leaving us with a legacy that can still be felt even today, nearly four decades on.

And we'll begin exploring that legacy in the next episode...

John Boden resides in the shadow of Three Mile Island with his wonderful wife and children. Aside from his work with *Shock Totem,* his stories can be found in *52 Stitches, Everyday Weirdness, Black Ink Horror #7,* and *Psychos: Serial Killers, Depraved Madmen, and the Criminally Insane,* edited by **John Skipp**.

Simon Marshall-Jones is a UK-based writer, artist, editor, publisher and blogger: also wine and cheese lover, music freak and covered in too many tattoos.

Fat Betty

by Harry Baker

They say it's God's own county, and He's always had a thing for rain. I'm high and soaked, looking over the valley with a sea of heather at my back, and if the storm lasts forty nights I'll not be shocked. There's still a little light over the hills to the east, but it's cloud-clogged overhead and the sunlight can't get through to where I'm huddled in anorak and hugging my carbine, praying for that bastard Jamie Cornfeld to make his way quick.

"You miserable sod," I tell him, when he comes up in his hood and coat with a rifle on his shoulder and a stick in his hand. "To meet up here." I might have walked down the street with gun in hands and not met an odd glance, let alone a copper.

"Do you good," he says, and he's right, although I'll not say it. "I guess that works, and all." He's looking at the carbine. Of course it works. Two tours and more Syrian sand than any crusader saw, it works all-bloody-right. One of them police half-tracks still has the holes.

"All right, then," he says, this being made clear, and we walk. It's that steady rain, not too heavy but sure to last all night, and the heather's wet, its springiness turned soggy. We scare some grouse and they go shooting off; I'd take a pot at them if we didn't need to keep quiet. Good eating on those birds, though I bet they were fatter when they were bred for it.

"Let's not fuss about this," I say. We've been walking five minutes, but it's been on my mind all day. "If there's trouble, we should shoot them."

"Yes," says Jamie. Good that he's not arguing. Jamie and me haven't worked on anything this big before. In fact, Jamie and me haven't partnered before, although we know each other from other odd jobs. I don't think he'd have approached me first, except that he knows I'm a safe pair of hands and that I don't like the Big Man.

We're quiet for a while longer as it gets dark, until I put my foot in a puddle. My boots aren't quite waterproof anymore.

"Shit," I say. "No weather for hiking."

"We have to walk up. They watch the roads," says Jamie, and he's right and I'm quiet once again. Up ahead there's something white sticking out of the heather, just showing through all the grey in the air. It's a short, rough-cut pillar, whitewashed for visibility, and up on top there's another rock, whitewashed as well, shaped like a circle or a square with its corners chipped off. A rough little cross, then. There are lots up here, old things, marking paths and parish boundaries. This one must have played signpost to travellers for centuries, before whatever line it marked got forgotten or grown over. It's a good sign. We're on track.

"You remember the road here?" Jamie asks me. "Not much sign of it now."

I don't remember (a little before my time), but my boot scuffs against a patch of tarmac, and with a bit of a squint I can see straight lines beneath the scrub. We follow them past the cross. Around the edge of the plinth there're moor flowers arranged almost like a pattern, and as we pass I see a mound of litter piled against the other side.

"Someone didn't clear their picnic," I say, joking, as if anyone would still picnic up here.

"No," says Jamie, shakes his head. I see what he means; it isn't even proper litter, but food still sealed in plastic, sopping wet supermarket and food-aid packaging. Weird that it was left up here, and I say so.

"It's traditional," says Jamie, with a sort of sneer. "A bite for Fat Betty." He says that last bit like it's a saying, or a nursery rhyme.

"What's that?" I ask.

"Something my nan used to say. Stupid bloody name for a cross." He presses on, not wanting to chat, maybe feeling a little odd talking about his nan with a gun on his back and murder on his mind. I take a moment to look: the cross isn't two stones at all but one big cross, with the top cut away and shaped. The carving has weathered right down, but there're circular hollows in the face of it and in one of them coins have been left, coppers and silver. I scoop those out and pocket them.

Jamie's seen me; he points and says "You reckon you'll need that after tonight?"

"It's a couple of cigarettes' worth," I tell him. "It adds up."

"My god," says Jamie. "I get lumbered with a penny-pincher for a job like this."

"Waste not want not," I say. "Don't sneer. It's an old-fashioned thing, sure, but you never know where the next pack's coming from."

Under the cloud the moors are rolling, and pretty soon we're walking along the old railway line where they hauled coal from the mines upon a time. There's a bump on the horizon just visible, which is the early-warning station at RAF Flyingdales, a great pyramid shape surrounded by barrack-blocks and razorwire. There's nothing worth shooting a nuclear missile at around here, but the big pyramid keeps turning slowly and there's a garrison of trigger-happy squaddies from London and Birmingham who lend muscle to the police when things get hairy. I don't like doing the job in sight of that place, but I don't say so. I reckon Jamie will have another sneer at me if I do.

The road coils down the hillside, very steep, and the slope beyond turns into a near-sheer escarpment down to the valley. We go into the middle of the road, the steepest bit, and from his bag Jamie takes a saucepan lid with the plastic handle removed. He puts it carefully in the centre of the road and shifts grit and mud to hold it in place on the slope.

"You take this side," he says, and goes up onto the escarpment. I find the ditch we picked out earlier: the tarp comes out of my anorak and over my head. I wait. It's darkening. I can't see the early-warning station any more.

It's a Friday night. Every Friday night the Big Man comes driving over the moor with the takings from the games. He lives on the farm near Stockdale, fortified so that even the police would have a headache going in, but his games need players and so they have to take place nearer the main roads. Being a tight git, he likes to carry the money himself, and Jamie Cornfeld knows the route because he worked for the Big Man right up until the unpleasantness at Pickering, which is itself a story long but worth the telling, some other time.

"He's a sick bugger," he told me in the pub when he floated the idea. "Even the bossmen don't like him. No one will fuss if we lift his winnings."

Of course, it's not that simple. The Big Man does nasty things to people who cross him. They end up as part and parcel of those games he plays, games where the participants finish dead or maimed and the watchers place their bets and the Big Man makes a killing, in every bloody sense of the word. We are diving in at the deep end, but then times have been hard for a little too long to be cautious.

I hear engines after twenty minutes, if my watch is right. This road's pretty clear most nights, and we'd reckoned rightly that the Big Man would be the first to come this way. When I peer out of the ditch I see lights and behind them two four-by-fours, a Land Rover up front and then a luxury model behind, both slowing to come down the slope. The bodyguards in the first car are probably ex-Army because they're good enough to spot the saucepan lid which, covered in dirt and in the dark, looks for all the world like the kind of improvised landmine they saw too many of in Iran. They stop, and because they're good they start reversing immediately, and the driver of the luxury car is good too because he realises what's happening straight away and is starting to do the same thing when Jamie throws the real bomb.

It's our one grenade, and he's cooked it so that it explodes as it bounces from the reversing Land Rover. Then there's fire and broken glass in the rain. I stand up in the ditch and put a burst into the fancy car. The carbine kicks my shoulder and the driver's window shatters. Like a sensible man he stops.

I run. Then, down on my knee, closer, in the heather, and it turns out I'm not too wet to feel the sloppy mud through my jeans. A muzzle flashes on the road up ahead. Fuck that. My sights line up like a beauty on the wrecked Land Rover as the first bodyguard comes out shooting; I move with him and tap the trigger smooth so that he twists and reels and flops into the water on the road. Bang-bang from Jamie Cornfeld up on the hill, and an answering burst of fire from behind the Land Rover. Jamie is moving up to the very edge of the escarpment now, overlooking the road, and he fires down. I guess he kills the fellow, because that's the end of it. I pull my balaclava on, and when I reach the fancy car, the driver is sitting and holding a hole in his shoulder, covered in blood and glass.

"You bastard," he says, level. I pull him out and push him into the road, take away the pistol he hasn't reached for and throw it into the gorse. Jamie comes down, all excited beneath his mask.

"Good work," he says. "Pity we had to kill them," but I can tell he's high on the fighting. Then we pull the Big Man out of his car, shouting all the time. There're two girls in the back with him, not overdressed because it's a heated car, and we haul them out as well to shiver a bit in the rain.

"You stupid bastards," says the Big Man. "You'll catch hell for this."

After all the stories and rumours I'm expecting him to be something else, but he's just a fat man with a boxer's flattened face. He goes on with the threats right up until Jamie puts the end of the rifle into his great bloated gut and knocks the breath from him so I can take his watch without fuss. The rain is washing all the blood away from the dead men in the road and I go through their pockets for their wallets. No hurry, after all, and no sense in leaving good money on the ground. Jamie takes the Big Man's briefcase and opens it. There's a lot more money there.

"Bingo," he says, and starts transferring it into the waterproof holdall on his back. I get a necklace from one of the girls. She tries a sort of smile and asks if she can keep it, but although she looks pretty with wet hair I'm not one to fall for it, and she's not one to make fuss without hope.

"You sit tight, sweetheart," I tell her. "We'll be gone before you know it."

"I'm cold," she says.

"Spare coat just there," I say, and nod at one of the dead men. She's quiet at that, and then she says "He's a cop," in a voice that's halfway between an admission and a taunt.

"Don't joke," I tell her, but there's a nasty lurch in my gut.

"Fuck you," she says. "They're Special Branch. He's—" she jerks her wet hair at the Big Man "—he's testifying."

"You stupid slut," says the Big Man. Jamie kicks him hard. Then he goes and looks at the bodies.

"They don't have cop guns," he says when he gets back. "But you don't know which Special Branch."

He sucks his teeth. If the dead men are coppers it'll mean armoured car patrols and doors kicked in and houses searched. It might mean there's backup on the way already. I look up at the road and imagine that I hear engines over the rain.

"We should move—" I start to say, but then there's a crack of gunshot behind me and I turn around to see that Jamie has just shot the Big Man in the head. The girl gasps, and then she starts to cry. I reckon that it's shock more than sorrow, but I don't bother asking.

"You didn't say you were going to do that," I say to Jamie.

"I wouldn't if it had gone smooth," he says. He's looking at the girls, wondering what to do about them.

"None of that," I say. "They didn't see anything, did you?"

I don't get an answer.

"Did you?" I say, a little louder.

"No," says the crying girl. She's shivering, wrapping her arms around her little cocktail dress.

"There," I say, stepping away. Jamie shakes his head, pulls me a little further off so we can't be heard.

"I don't like it," he says. "Two witnesses—"

"Three," I say.

"What do you mean, three?" says Jamie, snappish.

"The driver's still alive," I say.

"I know he is," says Jamie, and he looks at me oddlike.

"And the two girls makes three," I say. Jamie's face is a real picture.

"There's only one girl," he says.

"The hell there is," I say. His face isn't funny anymore; it's almost scary, and I turn, and there's one shivering girl with wet hair standing in the road.

"Fuck," I say, and I dash to the other side of the luxury car. The driver is sitting there, bleeding and looking bad.

"You bastard," he says again.

"Where'd she go?" I ask him.

"You bastard."

I go back the other side. Jamie is holding the briefcase in one hand and his gun in the other. He doesn't look happy.

"Where's your friend?" I ask the girl. Maybe I shout. I'm rattled.

"Please," she says, and looks at Jamie.

"The hell's wrong with you?" he says to me.

"She's can't be far," I say. "She must be in the heather, she can't be far—"

"Alex—" he says.

"It's you shooting the man," I tell him. "Scared her off."

"Mister," says the girl. "Mister, it was just me. Me and..." She looks at the Big Man's body and gulps. The rain has washed all the tears and mascara off her face. "Me and him."

"Get back in the car," says Jamie to the girl. She doesn't need telling twice. The door closes.

"There were two girls," I say. "There was her, and—"

But I can't remember what the quiet girl looked like. What she was wearing. What colour her hair was. I remember she didn't have any jewellery.

"Christ," I say. And although this is a horrible place to go mad, I see the funny side almost straight away and I giggle just a little. Jamie doesn't like it.

"For God's sake, pull yourself together," he says.

"I saw her," I tell him. "I must have eaten something weird." Funny how that's the first thing I think of, like my mum would have done.

"Come on," he snaps, but then there's an engine suddenly audible over the rain and the first police Land Rover comes over the hill with its lights blazing like eyes.

We shoot at it. Then we run. It's one of those things that needs no discussion at all. The Land Rover veers off to the side of the road and a second comes past it, breaks screaming, pulling over. We go off the road and they don't risk following in the cars. Instead they spill out and chase us, and when the first shots are fired good soldierly instinct takes over and we cover each other in turn, shooting high to make them keep their heads down. Our carbines have them out-ranged, and we're waist-deep in heather, hard to see in all this rain. We don't panic. I'm a long way from feeling my best, but panic is what kills at moments like this, and I'm not planning to wind up dead.

I shout and point to Jamie and we cut downhill towards the village and the network of lanes and hedges and fields that will shield us for at least a while. I start to think ahead as I fumble for a fresh clip. They will have squads blocking off the roads before long, which means we're in for a long walk tonight if we're to make it home, and with no guarantee of safe haven at the end of it. But they're not following us close and the rain's getting worse. For once that's good. Jamie points this time, and we go straight down the hill into the valley, running and then sliding on our arses when it gets too steep. A bullet smacks the mud near my hand, but it must be a fluke shot because nothing else I see comes close and as the slope levels out halfway down the police above are out of sight.

I get up. "Come on," I say to Jamie, and he gurgles something because there's a big hole in his neck, where a copper's lucky bullet has gone through as we slid.

"Jamie," I say. He's left blood in all the muddy tracks we made, and he's dead from the loss of it almost as soon as I've said that one word. I take the holdall heavy with money and ease the strap over his wet body and onto my shoulder. It's a pity. It happens.

I run. I have to get off the slope, where any bugger with eyes can see me, but I'm soaked and weighted down and out of breath before I know it, and as I stagger back into the heather I'm trusting the night and the weather to keep me from being seen. It's all close, the rain thick and burdensome. I'm freezing, but I've got the money and I've got the gun, and those two things make me feel like I can make it right up until the point when I bang my hand against something.

"Fuck," I say, my knuckles bloody, and then I look and see the rough-cut whitewashed stone cross we passed before. I say the word again, and realise that I really am going mad because this cross was high on the moor, back the way we came, and I haven't gone an inch uphill since Jamie died.

It's a different cross, I think. It just looks the same. There are plenty up here. This is another good sign. But I know I'm wrong. It's whitewashed in the same way, and those same offerings of food and flowers are laid out—I recognise the bright sopping wet plastic packaging, and oh God but I'm spooked by that. I walk quickly away, back towards the spot where I waited for Jamie, and the overgrown tarmac of the old road scuffs under my boots. The rain is heavy. I can't hear the cops. I can't even see lights from the road behind me, and this spot wasn't far from there. My hand hurts.

This happens. I zone out. I probably climbed up here to throw the cops off and didn't even notice, I was thinking so hard about it. The firefights in the desert used to work like that, during my service—all action and I couldn't remember how it happened afterwards.

But I always remembered that it *had* happened.

This rain! And up ahead, lights appear out of it, car lights on the road—and it's the road I left with Jamie, the road with the Big Man's cars static in it and the cops just cresting the hill to come down on us.

That road is behind me.

I swear to God, that road is behind me.

I can hear my teeth chatter. No surprise, I've been in the rain too long. It's cold. Not much visibility. I have walked in a circle; that is what I have done. It is not surprising in this weather. This weather is why I haven't been caught yet.

Oh God.

I haven't been caught because there are no cops on this road, no sign of them. And that's fucked up, that's all wrong: there were two cop cars when we ran, big Land Rovers with reinforced glass in the windows.

I turn my back on the road. They drove off, I tell myself. No they bloody didn't, myself tells me right back. Then I catch a glimpse.

It's her, the quiet one from the car. I know it's her although I only get the briefest of looks at her, out in the heather up to her waist, standing still. Then I blink, or maybe I just don't want to look any more, but anyway she's lost in the night and I'm doubtful for a second that I saw anything.

I'm going fucking mad. I want more than anything to see a cop, so I must be mad. You know where you are with cops. I walk again. I probably walk in another bloody circle.

Next time I see her, she's closer, and she's different somehow. Something about her face. Her wet hair's all against it, a tangle, like the gorse at my feet. She's just there watching as I lumber through the heather with bag and carbine, and she looks down when I see her.

Screw this, I think, and I call to her.

"I'm not going to hurt you," I say. "I'm only lost. Are you lost too?" I don't know what she's doing out here, and I tighten my grip on the carbine. But maybe she is only lost. "I won't hurt you," I tell her again.

She has something in her hand, and she flicks it around her fingers like a conker on a string. It's the Big Man's watch. I feel the pocket I'd put it in, and it's gone. I must have lost it somewhere on the moors.

"Where'd you get that?" I say, and she looks at me straight. There's something jagged about her face.

"Love," I say to her. "Love, what the hell's happening?"

She opens her mouth. Opens it wide.

I don't want to talk about that.

So then I'm running again. I'm running and I've stopped caring that my lungs hurt and my soaked, tired body is aching, because I'm scared like I've never been scared by people just shooting at me. I have a sense now, an intuition, that I've crossed someone very old and very powerful, bigger than the Big Man ever was.

The carbine swings on its strap, and it's leaving bruises on my hip and thigh where it hits. It's not a comfort any more. Bullets won't make a blind bit of bloody difference to any of this. I feel as though I am the only human thing on this moor, alone, high above the valley with nothing but rain and blackness for miles and maybe across the whole world. I know even as I'm running that I won't get anywhere, and when that squat ugly white-washed stone cross looms out of the heather again I know I'm done and I just stop.

She stands up from where she's been crouched, where she must have been crouched, and now she's short and stocky, and very very pale. I can't tell what she's wearing, or what her face is like; I just know that she's the same, that she's *Her*, the shape detaching itself from the whitewashed rock and making little steps towards me. I can see a smear of blood on the cross where my knuckle cracked against it. The rain should have washed it off by now. In her hand she has a piece of bright plastic, a supermarket chocolate bar left on the stone. She is eating it, wrapper and all, in small deliberate bites, slicing it with her sharp teeth and not really swallowing. A bite for Fat Betty, Jamie's nan used to say—and he's right, it is a stupid bloody name, because she's not fat at all. She's just eaten a lot.

I think there are tears soaking into the balaclava on my face, tears and rain and sweat. She eats the last of the chocolate and then reaches out and pulls the mask off me—right off, the material stretching and ripping as she tugs it. I'm almost too cold to feel it.

"Please," I say. I take hold of the carbine, but I don't pull the trigger. I think that nothing will happen if I do, and if I prove myself right that will be the end of me. She's got a face like cut marble. It isn't a human face. I don't know how I thought that she was a person. When she speaks, her lips barely part, and her voice is like something that's been dead a long time.

"Didn't your mother teach you not to steal?"

It's a funny thing to say. I would have thought I'd laugh if anyone had said that to me in earnest. Laughing is the last thing I want to do now.

"I never took anything from you," I say. "I swear to God—" and I hold up my hands, the bag full of blood money swinging off one arm and the murderous carbine off the other "—I never took nothing of yours."

She steps towards me. I back away, scrabble in my pocket; the carbine slips and I let it fall into the heather so I can haul out the necklace I took from the other girl.

"This is your friend's," I say. "I didn't take yours."

I throw it to her. She treads it into the scrub. Then I'm opening the big bag and holding it out, full of the Big Man's banknotes, rain smacking into the paper. I drop the bag and the money spills out to spoil in the wet undergrowth. She keeps coming, and I'm stumbling and wrecked.

"That's it," I say. "Please. What do you want?"

She stops, and it seems to me that she is at once high above me and very close. She isn't anything I can describe. She holds out a hand. I don't have anything to put in it, and I stand and shiver silent. She catches my belt and pulls me close, and for a stupid second I think the awful thought that she's going to kiss me. Instead, she puts a hand into the pocket of my jeans and rips it so that the coins spill out, a couple of cigarettes worth if you add them up, tumbling into the dirt, the coins I took from her cross.

It's traditional, Jamie Cornfeld said.

~

They find me just there, when it's beginning to get light. Maybe police, maybe soldiers; it's been years since I served and they look more and more like each other nowadays. I'm on my back, spread-eagled, the soaked, ruined banknotes strewn all about me, the bag empty in the heather a few yards off. I come awake when they kick me, feverish with cold and wet and my head aching something terrible.

I don't say anything to them. I look past them at the stone cross, which sits in the heather as squat and ugly as it ever was. The blood from my hand has washed away overnight. I wanted to be sure of that, though for a moment I don't know why.

"You bastard," says one of them, an officer. "What the hell were you on?"

I'm hauled up and cuffed, knocked about a bit. The usual. It wakes me up.

"You messed up, mate," the officer says. "You left witnesses."

I must look blank, because he laughs in a way I don't like. I remember shooting and a road, and the Big Man dead in it, but it doesn't feel important.

"You're still high, aren't you?" he says. "You must have been like a bloody kite when you crashed out up here. Might have got clear if you'd kept going."

He pushes me, not too hard. Jamie's dead, I remember. I should feel sad about that, sometime.

"Come on," he says. "Let's move."

We walk single file, back towards the road and their vehicles. The torn pocket of my jeans is flapping against my leg. As we pass the cross, I look at it and I see the little circular hollows carved into it, like eyes in a face. There's a little pile of coins stacked in one of them, the lowest, between the others, a great gaping mouth in the ugly misshapen face. There's just enough money there for a couple of cigarettes. Old fashioned, yes, but then she was more than old fashioned; she was old, as old as that stone and as set in the land. This is her place.

They will hang me for what I have done.

I hope they do it a long way from here.

Harry Baker grew up in North Yorkshire and Peterborough, and is currently studying at the London Film School. This is his first published story.

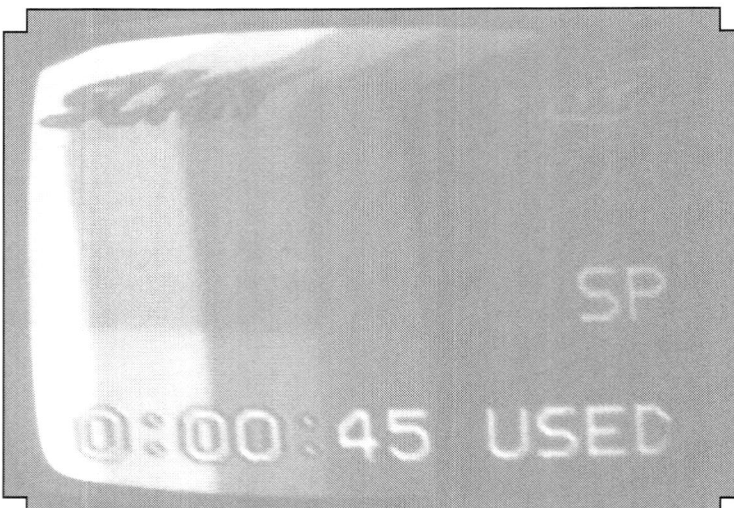
SP
0:00:45 USED

Until I'm Dead
A Conversation with Adam Cesare

by K. Allen Wood

In my mind, two distinct things stand out when I think of Adam Cesare.

Adam was one of the first to review our debut issue. *Hellfire Right Out of the Gate* was the review title. In simpler words: he liked it. We met in person shortly thereafter at Rock and Shock, a horror-meets-music convention held annually in Worcester, Massachusetts. What I remember most about that day is how he seemed genuinely excited to meet me, *Shock Totem*'s publisher and editor. Maybe my ego interpreted things incorrectly, but all I know is that that was the first time I felt like we were truly doing something special, maybe even something great. Today I consider Adam a friend, but he was just a fan then, someone who was enthusiastic about what we were doing, and that meant a lot.

That was five years ago, and now we've come full circle, to where I am *his* fan.

In the last few years, Adam has gone from aspiring author to *inspiring* author. Truly, I've had the pleasure of watching him progress from a writer with potential to one who wields words with great strength and power. Whether it's Adam Cesare or Mercedes M. Yardley or Lee Thompson, being present to witness that kind of metamorphosis—a spark become a flame become a raging firestorm—has been one of the greatest rewards of publishing *Shock Totem*.

And so it is my pleasure to present to you this conversation with the man himself. Hail, Cesare!

~

KW: Adam, welcome. Thanks for taking the time to answer a few questions.

AC: Thanks for having me. Longtime listener, first-time caller.

KW: I recently finished your collection with Matt Serafini, *All-Night Terror*, and your latest release, *The First One You Expect*. I'm also in the middle of *The Summer Job* (yeah, I know; I read too many books at once). What is immediately clear, is how far you've come since *Tribesmen*, how much stronger your prose is. How happy are you with your progress and success thus far?

AC: I'm reading through like five books now myself between paperbacks and pre-reading and my kindle, so I can empathize.

Yeah, I do think I've gotten better and I'm very happy with that. Happy but never fully satisfied, right? It's like every page makes you stronger, pushes you along but you don't want to repeat yourself so you get complacent. The goal is to keep that trajectory going for a whole bunch of decades, until I'm dead.

KW: What's your process like? Do you start with an idea and just roll with it, let the story unravel organically; or do you outline?

AC: Most of the publishers I work with have required synopses that take the story from beginning to end and at first I really hated that.

From what I see on Facebook, etc. I think it's like the 'cool' thing to do, to hate that The Man is forcing you to work from a synopsis, but if you want to write for these places you have to learn to enjoy the process and I definitely have.

Only *Tribesmen* and *Video Night* were written without a synopsis, which offered all the freedom in the world but also led to moments (especially on *Video Night*) where I had to backtrack and tangle with some real mechanical problems with the narrative. If you go into a book with a malleable but still fully-functioning outline, you don't run into those problems and you can focus on the writing itself.

For *The Summer Job* I wrote a fairly extensive, high-detail outline and I think it allowed me to write a richer, more complicated book than I would have been able to do without one. Not to give anything away, but it's a book where a lot of the tension comes from dramatic irony, the reader keeping tabs on what characters know what, but still never having the full picture until the very end. That's not to say that every little thing was planned in advance (the whole third act is different than the outline, and *way* better, I think), but it's nice to have a provisional blueprint.

I'm writing another complicated thing right now and if the publisher hadn't insisted on an outline I would have clawed my eyes out by now.

KW: So you're able to be objective enough to know when the outline isn't working and just kind of toss it and jam?

AC: With me it's never so much a case of not working as it is all the little deviations I make from the outline add up to the story moving in a new direction. That's why it usually happens late in a project. But yeah, if I'm in a corner I can jam.

KW: One surprising thing about your writing, given how young you are, is that it's a very classic style of storytelling, deeply rooted in the 70s and 80s. In the hands of a lesser writer this would come off as pastiche, but your work reads exceedingly genuine, even more authentic than the work of many who directly experienced those eras. Besides an obvious love and appreciation of the time period, particularly in the creative realms, how are you able to so

convincingly fool us all?

AC: Thank you.

Well, I used to be big into doing period pieces. *Tribesmen* takes place in the early 1980s, when films were still very much products of the seventies and *Video Night* being late-eighties, anticipating the nineties. So when I was doing those my philosophy was think like the characters, not like someone who was writing patter for one of those VH1 *I Love the 80s* shows.

If I referenced something (which I do sparingly in *Tribesmen*, given the characters and setting), I didn't want it to read like name-dropping, just a natural expression of that character's interests and goals at that point in the story. I think these cultural nods might read a little more broadly in *Video Night*, not only because it's the first thing I wrote, but because those characters are so invested in the media they consume.

Because my first two books employed that trick, afterwards I wanted to do some stories that took place in present day. The funny thing is I guess I can't get away from those themes, nostalgia-addled characters, because the protagonist in *The Summer Job* is informed/haunted by her high school days, the struggles she faces trying to reinvent herself for college and then beyond that, once she graduates. *Zero Lives Remaining* also takes place in 2014, but it's set in a video arcade, something we don't have many of these days. The protagonist there is obsessed with games that are a decade-plus older than she is.

None of these characters are much like me, so to "fool" people I try that trick that magicians employ: most illusions only look good if your audience is standing at a really specific angle to you. I try to find tiny details that I may not have firsthand experience with, but are specific enough (and researched well enough) to read as true, when placed within the context of my "act."

KW: You're a student of film and have a true love for cinema, which is quite evident in your work. In the past, you've worried about being pigeonholed as a "cinematic" writer. Why is that? And are you ready to accept that maybe it's just part of your writer DNA?

AC: I think I've worried more about being the guy who writes about movies, not maybe so much having a "cinematic" style. People say that of me and I get where they're coming from, a bit, but I'm kind of myopic when it comes to my own style and can't judge it. Maybe "cinematic" is just a nice way of saying I write too literally, although I hope not.

I admire the way people like Laird Barron write, him and the other more "classical" writers of weird fiction, and I've experimented trying to ape stuff like that, but I like writing like me, what comes naturally. As long as, like we said in the beginning of this interview, I can keep sharpening that sword, doing it better with each book.

I returned to the subject of horror cinema recently with *The First One You Expect*, which is a noir, a crime book set in the world of DIY horror movies. That one is tonally different than my other film-based fiction, WAY darker. Film is a big subject and I really don't think I'll be running out of aspects of it to talk about anytime soon, I'll write about it when I think of the projects and sometimes I won't. I like mixing it up.

KW: Sure, you can't write about movies or movie culture all the time, but surely you can write in a style tailor-made *for* movies. If that makes sense. And that doesn't suggest a simpler, more literal style, lacking depth. Stephen King, I think, writes from that "cinematic" base.

AC: Probably has to do with the way I think, maybe how deep down cinematic language has sunken into my brain. I'm a big reader, I'm very proud of that. I try to read as widely as possible, inside and outside the genre, highbrow and lowbrow, but still movies are my first love, so that informs not only the way I write, but the way I think.

I will say: If I write *for* movies, then where are all my options? Please make all checks payable to cash.

KW: Patience!

You're a recent transplant to Philadelphia via Boston via New York. Over the years I've noticed a striking number of people—authors, artists, filmmakers, actors—in the horror field hail from Pennsylvania. How different from Boston and New York is the Philly scene?

AC: I was skeptical at first, I really love Boston, but Philly is great. I hang out with a few people who are into horror, there's a great community for both cinema and fiction. Really cool repertory shows, lots of used bookstores (though people tell me there used to be more). There's also a really cool convention a quick bus ride away in Jersey: Monster Mania, it happens twice a year, Shock Totem should come down for one.

KW: I remember when I first joined the Air Force and learned I was being stationed in Little Rock, Arkansas, I was convinced the scene was going to be

nonexistent or close to it. I was pleasantly surprised to find out that it was not only massive but *thriving*. From musicians to actors to writers to artists of all mediums. This scenario repeated itself as I traveled the globe.

AC: Just goes to show there are awesome people everywhere. It's part of why I like going to conventions, you hear lots of different accents, but they're all talking about their love of similar things.

KW: You self-published your digital collection *Bone Meal Broth*, but you're primarily publishing with a variety of small press publishers. While you're undoubtedly a rising star within the small press, have you begun setting your sights higher?

AC: Yeah, self-publishing is an amazing tool for people who can do it right. *Bone Meal* was an experiment in that, a cheap sample for people who weren't sure whether they wanted to pick up my traditionally published material. Most of the stories in there were published under another name in paying markets, so once I had the rights back I figured what the hell.

I just don't have the level of hustle that successful self-published authors have. I don't "cast a wide enough net" with my "online presence" in order to "further my brand."

KW: Self-promotion is an art unto itself. Most people come off as obnoxious spammers, while others do great with the social interaction and building a following but fail to engage those people beyond mutual disingenuous ego stroking. In both scenarios you have people who simply don't care about your work, the latter group just pretends to. Few people are able to build a large, genuine following that truly cares about their work.

AC: It's so hard. We all have to do it, and when I do I feel like I'm inflicting my garbage on people. And I end up feeling especially bad about it if I have nothing of value to say beyond "Buy my book!" I still do it, but I try to show some restraint.

Maybe that's the key, though, if you don't have Jiminy Cricket on your shoulder saying "I don't know champ, maybe you shouldn't invite them to 'like' your author page ten minutes after they accepted your request and have no clue who you are" you're liable to do it.

KW: What is your five- or ten-year plan?

AC: Five-year plan? Ten? Jeez, that's a lot of pressure. Yeah, I have my eyes on the prize and would love to get in with one of the big New York publishers, but I'm quite happy with the work I'm doing now and what I've got coming out with small/medium sized presses. In my short time publishing I've gotten to work with some of my heroes and I would like to keep doing that.

But if we're talking ultimate dream job stuff that is not the obvious work with one of the "Big Five" publishers? I'd love to write comics. I experimented with the format with my friend, artist Nick Lopergalo, and I think the results were awesome, a little twenty page women-in-prison-with-monsters one-shot called *The New Fish*.

KW: Is *The New Fish* something destined to remain in archives or will it be available at some point?

AC: It's something we're going to show around, but if nobody takes it, we'll still find a way for people to see it. When I'm proud of something, it's meant for public consumption.

Is Shock Totem interested?

KW: Well, Shock Totem Comics *does* have a nice ring to it.

This spring we're releasing your novella *Zero Lives Remaining*—which is brilliant, of course—but besides that, what else do you have planned over the coming months and years?

AC: I've had the good fortune of being able to collaborate with some writers I really respect. Cameron Pierce, Shane McKenzie, and I wrote a book called *Leprechaun in the Hood: The Musical: The Novel*. That was Cameron's idea, and it's as crazy and funny as the title suggests. We're looking to place that somewhere cool.

After that Shane invited me to work with him, Kristopher Rufty and David Bernstein on a book called *Jackpot*, which is about a serial killer who wins the lottery. That will be coming out soon in limited hardcover along with more affordable editions.

In November my next novel with Samhain should be dropping, that one's called *Exponential* and is a giant monster story, but done in a new way, I think.

And right now I'm working on my biggest book yet, something really special.

KW: Well, my friend, I'll let you get back to it, then. It goes without saying

that I'm looking forward to whatever you have a hand in writing. Thanks again, bud!

AC: Thank you, Ken. I look forward to this issue, as I do all of them.

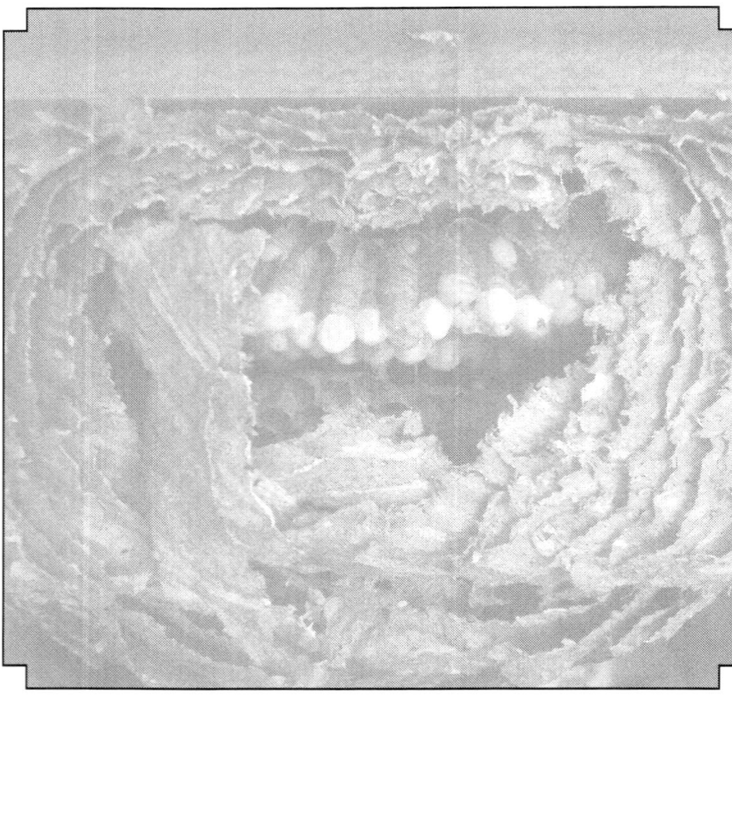

2013 Flash Fiction Contest Winner
STABAT MATER

by Michael Wehunt

Nolan found his wife crouched under the back deck, her swollen belly pressed against the soft dead leaves. He started to squat next to her but the sound of liquid pattering against the ground stopped him. For a frantic moment he thought her water had broken.

The smell hit him then, a heady sourness. Between Lily's bare feet came a thin creek of urine, trickling over her toes. She lowered her arms and he saw bits of leaves on her skin. They moved down toward her elbows. Not leaves but wasps, a dozen or so exploring her.

"Lily?" Nolan tried to reach out but couldn't. Panic surged over him, roaring in his ears vast and empty as the inside of a seashell. He was allergic to wasps and bees and all their kin. His EpiPen was in the upstairs bathroom but it was the phobia, its blind terror, that made him stagger back from her.

She shook her arms and the wasps lifted and vanished under the floor of the deck. Then she sidled out into the yard and stood, half-naked, rotted leaves clinging to the underside of her belly. She was due any day now. Their first child, at last, the name Elaine and her grandmother's antique crib waiting for her.

He snatched Lily's arms and searched for any lingering wasps. "You scared me," he said. His fingers came away grainy and sticky. "Lil, did you put sugar on your skin?"

"They're perfect creatures, really," she said, looking back toward the deck. "Each child is a copy of its mother."

"Did any get you?" He shook her, hated himself for it, but the panic was still close.

"Our baby should be perfect."

"She will be. She already is, honey. Come inside." He guided her up the deck steps. She remained pliant, like someone in shock, while he washed her and tucked her into bed.

He understood she was under a lot of pressure. They had struggled to get pregnant. But just as adoption had entered the vocabulary of their marriage, Lily had kindled. Her first two trimesters had been a smooth joy. Lily had a glow that drew smiles from strangers.

Before long she'd become a scholar of expectant motherhood, immersing herself with an intensity that might have seemed frightening to Nolan with any lesser ambition. She meditated. The house filled with organic cookbooks, Ashtanga yoga videos. Processed foods were verboten along with anything that dared to have gluten. Classical and ambient music drifted like clouds. Nolan cracked New Age and granola jokes.

But then she'd turned inward, distant and airy. She spoke of purity and perfection and didn't like being touched as often. Nolan knew that her mother had a daughter before Lily, a sad thing who'd died of SIDS in her crib. He couldn't get Lily to talk about it.

He waited until her breaths lengthened into what would eventually be her light whistling snores, then laid a hand on the globe of her belly. Elaine kicked his palm, eager to meet her papa. "A few more days, pumpkin," he whispered, and kissed his wife's hair.

He stood in the middle of the living room. Pärt's *Stabat Mater* mourned from the entertainment center. It had been on repeat these last few days, straining the house with its slow, lovely ache. There was a violence to it. Voices lamenting the sorrows of Mary, according to the CD's liner notes. And what more famous mother could there be, he asked himself, and shook the thought away.

Outside the light slipped into dusk. Nolan bent and with a flashlight swept the underside of the deck. The nest was the size of a small plate. A carpet of wasps shifted over it, sluggish with night. How could this happen? He was vigilant with the house, hiring an exterminator in the warm months.

He brushed at himself with a shudder. His skin crawled with phantom prickles.

~

He came home the next day and searched the house for Lily, finally finding her in the basement's farthest corner, among cobwebs and the reek of urine. The doors of her mother's china cabinet were open and she stood gazing into it, naked, her pale hair fanning across her shoulders. Small black shapes flitted through the gloom. A wasp passed in front of him and he shrieked, slapping at his face.

"Lily, get away from there," he said, ashamed at the harsh tremble in his voice. The EpiPen had been in his back pocket all day but still he was frozen in place, unable to step near his wife. His mind funneled back to his sixth summer, a week in the hospital after digging near a yellow jacket nest. Thirty years and he still felt shaped by that day. He remembered how the ground had exhaled them in a great humming breath. There hadn't even been time to stand up.

"Come and rescue me," she called across to him. Her voice carried a lilt. "They really are perfect little things. Fearless."

But he couldn't. Another wasp droned past his ear. He fled upstairs and stuffed a towel under the basement door, shaking and cursing himself.

~

She went into labor two days early, soaking the mattress as dawn streaked the bedroom curtains. An overnight bag had been in the car since last week, and in two minutes he had her dressed and outside.

Wasps were everywhere. Saucers, bowls, coffee mugs sat on the steps and the porch railing, covered with the insects and smears of honey that caught the strengthening light.

"Why would you do this?" he whispered.

She didn't answer. Nolan stood rooted in his fear through several of her contractions. The EpiPen was miles away in the bedroom. Spots swarmed in his vision. Lily groaned in pain. He bit his tongue and lifted her and tried not to fall down the steps.

A wasp landed on the back of his neck. He forced himself forward. By the time he reached the car it had flown away.

~

He could never have imagined a more beautiful thing than Elaine. Seven pounds, five ounces of wailing health, a bundle of heaven in his wife's arms. Lily wouldn't quite look at the baby, but she was smiling. If the smile was hesitant, it was because the labor had worn her out, that was all. Nolan took that smile and held it, almost like a second infant. He looked down at what they had made and felt himself fill with light.

As a gesture to Lily—that Elaine would have a brave father—he killed the wasps on his own rather than call the exterminator. He wrapped himself in winter clothes and scoured every nook and cranny. It took a couple of bug bombs and six cans of spray, but soon the house was ready for his family.

He slept little that first night with Elaine home. The baby fussed between them in the bed, and Lily turned away from her, facing the corner of the room. Nolan cooed to Elaine, whispering that Mama was just tuckered out from bringing her into the world.

It was worth every yawn the next day. The office was a sort of prison and his parole didn't come through until after six. It seemed he caught every red light on the way home.

"How are my two girls doing?" he said the moment he stepped through the door. Lily sat in his recliner beneath a blanket. The *Stabat Mater* was just ending, fading within the speakers.

"Nothing's perfect enough the first time." She looked at him and something in her face made him step back. "You understand."

"Where's Elaine?" His throat dried up. "What did you do?"

"The next one will be just right. It's not your fault you gave her your weakness."

She pulled down a corner of the blanket. Nolan saw an arm, shiny and red and swollen. A wasp wandered up over the wrist and disappeared within the tiny fingers.

Michael Wehunt's fiction has appeared or is forthcoming in such publications as *Cemetery Dance*, *Shadows & Tall Trees*, and *One Buck Horror*, among others. This is his second story to appear in *Shock Totem*. He spends his time in the lost city of Atlanta. Please visit him at www.michaelwehunt.com.

Depresso the Clown

by John Skipp

It's a rancid corn dog breakfast again. She slides it under the door, on the unwashed plastic tray. The note on the tray says GOOD MORNING, FREAK! Otherwise, I'd have no way of knowing.

There are no windows in this basement. No light but the jittering fluorescents overhead. Forever on. Forever just out of reach. Like the door. The walls. The many sharp and painful objects.

All the other things they've kept hidden from the world.

I awake on the cold concrete, face as far from the drain as the chains will allow. And my face is ablaze with smoldering pain, like a million tiny insect stings. I swat at it with my padded hands, but that only makes it worse.

I try to say something, but I no longer can.

I hear her laugh, as she heads back up the stairs. And that sound, more than anything, brings the burning tears again. There is no surgery short of death that can keep my soul from sobbing.

"Aw, poor baby," she says. "Now THAT'S funny!"

Then I'm alone with my sorrow, my corn dog, and pain.

~

I wish I could remember the date exactly. The twenty-somethingth of August of this year. It was hot, I can tell you that. So hot my makeup was running. I was on break between shows, catching a quick smoke out back, when this guy came walking up and said, "Hey."

"Hey," I said back, not really looking, scoping out the less-than-half-empty parking lot. Not a whole lot of people that day. Business had been in the crapper for years, was not getting any better.

"You get high?" he said, and that got my attention. I'd been nursing my last gram of Sour Cheese Deisel for over a week. Rob kept saying he'd score for sure in the next town, but it just kept not happening. And we were days out from medico-legal Michigan.

"You're talkin' weed, right?" I said.

"I'm talkin' whatever you want." He grinned, showing godawful teeth. He had the scrawny scarecrow look of a third-string high school basketball player who found crack and then woke up ten years later, still wearing the same t-shirt.

Any fear that he might be an undercover cop vanished right there. Just another local loser, working us like we worked them.

"Well, hell," I said, "I could use a quick toke."

He proffered a skinny-ass joint from his pocket. "Van's right over there, if that's cool."

I looked, saw several parked within a hundred yards. "That's cool. Appreciate it."

And off we went.

It's weird, how clearly I remember that final trek across the dirt and gravel. How loud everything sounded. How alert my senses felt. It was like I was stoned already, walking beside him, the sun angled in just such a way that his tall man shadow draped over me. Like his smile was suddenly my umbrella. I remember thinking that, and being mildly amused.

But was I scared? Not even a little. I just wished I was wearing different shoes, different clothes, wasn't dressed for work. Didn't want any grief when I got back. Didn't need any busybody shit. When I looked around and saw nobody, my only thought was, "Oh, thank God."

We passed a van, came up on another, its bashed-in front grill pointed toward us. This got my hopes up, but we walked alongside it without stopping or slowing. The next van was a good fifty yards away. I started to get concerned.

"I'm back on in fifteen minutes, just to be clear," I said.

"Uh-huh," he said, just as we reached the back of the van.

I heard him stop, a split-second before I did.

And there she was, beside the open back door.

I took in the bleached blond hair, bulging halter top, cut-off jeans at hot-pants length. Saw the dimpled legs and beer-bloat midriff, almost rivaling her boobs. Saw the garish trailer tramp makeup, red lips so huge and crudely drawn they looked clownish themselves. Saw her crappy tattoos.

But mostly what I noted was her terror, at the sight of me. The high-beam crazy of her eyes.

"Omigod! Omigod! HIT HIM, JERRY!" she screamed.

This he did. From behind.

That was my last glimpse of sky.

~

I ain't afraid of you...

The world came back to me, black and cold, throbbing with pain and something worse underneath. I felt it before I felt the floor, heard the faint clink of metal so close to my ears. I felt it in my bones, like they'd been first to awaken.

You can't scare me no more...

That feeling was doom.

It was in me before my eyes flickered open, saw the harsh strobing light and squeezed shut again. It was soaked into my bones before I could smell the dankness, taste the concrete and dust on my tongue.

"Ever since I was little," droned the little girl voice, coming in clearer as my senses caught up, "I been petrified of you. Like I couldn't even move, I felt so frickin' helpless and scared..."

I groaned and stirred, felt the tug and the weight, the clamps tight around my wrists.

"I would wake up from nightmares, and you would be there. Still there. Like the dream coughed you up, left you hangin' up over my bed. Lookin' down. Lookin' down at me and laughin'."

"Oh, no, no," I croaked, more reflex than intention.

"But them days are over. Ain't gonna be like that no more."

I opened my eyes, saw the shackles on my polka-dot sleeves. Saw the shiny red ridge of the squeezable ball on the tip of my nose.

And it all came horribly clear.

"Oh, no, no, no," I said, rising up with a clatter. Rising up only as high as my knees before the chains went taut and yanked me back. I looked around. Saw the chains. Saw the bars of my cage.

Saw the girl recoil, as I faced her at last.

"I AIN'T AFRAID OF YOU!" she shrieked in her little girl squeak, though she had to be thirty at least.

"No, no, no!" I yelled back. "C'mon! You gotta be kiddin'! I mean, what the fuck did *I* do?"

"Oh, you *know* what you did!"

"I didn't do *anything*, lady! I ride a fucking unicycle! I get hit in the face with pies! I give out balloons to kids! Not monster balloons! Just regular ones!"

"Jerry?" she screeched, gaze flailing everywhere but me.

"Honest to God, I make less than you make if you work at Wal-Mart! I have no power over anyone! My life is total shit!"

"Jerry!" In a panic now.

"I mean, Christ! I was probably just out of high school when you saw Stephen King's 'It', or whatever the fuck happened! But lemme tell you something: CIRCUS CLOWNS ARE JUST PEOPLE! We just wanna make you laugh! It's a job, fercrissake!"

I heard footsteps thunder down the stairs, like two bowling balls racing each other. For one measly moment, I entertained hope. Maybe cops. A nice S.W.A.T. team or three.

"JERRY"

"I'm comin', baby!" called the voice I feared most.

And that was that. So much for hope. I caught my reflection on the shackle on my wrist, saw the white face and red lips, my own warped and desperate eyes.

"Dude!" I hollered. "PLEASE! Come on! It's just me! We were gonna get high!"

I brought my sleeve up, wiped the makeup from one cheek. It came off in a greasepaint smear.

"See? *This is not my face!*"

"JERRY!"

"I'm just a guy! We probably like the same movies! *Look!*" I rubbed my other cheek pink, popped the ball off my nose.

Jerry hit the cage door running.

Then he came in, and cut out my tongue.

~

I cry all the time now. It's pretty much what I do. Cry and whimper, scream and moan. I spend most of my time in the fetal position, while my mind races and my body quakes.

I think about all the things I never did. All the places I never went, and never will. All the girls I never kissed. All the jokes I never made. All the weed I never smoked. On and on and on and on.

Sometimes, I helplessly fantasize about about my missing person report. Imagine someone's looking for me. That's the cruelest one of all. I was a transient before I joined the circus. Guys like me come and go, from job to job. One day we show up and audition. A little juggling, a couple pratfalls, and we're on the team. From there, we hang in for as long as it's good, often vanish just as quickly as we came.

I'm not saying they didn't notice me gone, and maybe even miss me a little. I'm just sayin' odds are good that nobody thought, "Someone kidnapped our clown in the parking lot," and put out an APB.

Thinking these thoughts just drives the doom in deeper.

The only close-to-good thoughts are of death, or revenge.

Every day, she comes down and faces her demon. The fact that I'm not one was always way beside the point. It's a matter of pride for her. To see me so weak makes her feel strong.

I'm her totem. Her placebo. Her triumph of the will. I'm the surrogate for everyone that ever wronged her, every Evil Clown movie she ever saw. I'm the reason for her baby-voiced arrested development. The source of all her soul's scar tissue.

And she is making me pay for it all.

That's where Jerry comes in.

The first thing he did after cutting out my tongue was to sew that rubber ball back on the end of my nose. "Nuh-uh-uh," he said, grinning, as the needle dug in. "You don't get off that easy."

Then he carefully affixed these massively-padded Mickey Mouse gloves to my wrists with fishing wire, careful not to pop a vein. So that my fingers were buried inside those four cartoon fingers, unable to pry the stitching loose, Fight back. Or tear my own throat out, as the case may be.

She has me all day, to drop in on at will, in between whatever snacks, sex toys, and reality TV she wiles away the rest on. Insofar as I can tell, she never leaves the damn house.

But at night, Jerry comes home. And I am his project.

Every night, after work, he drags me back to the chair.

Every night, he tattoos a little more of my face.

He could have done it all at once, but he's taking his time. This is clearly his favorite part of the day. Just the white took two months. He spent three weeks on the lips. Now he's rouging my cheeks. And I know the eyes are next.

Fuck if I don't spend every second in that chair just wanting to kill him, over and over. Him and his stupid girlfriend. I wrap the chains around their necks. I stick the needles in their eyes. I taunt, torment, and torture them. Eye for eye. Nose for nose. Limb for limb. Cell by cell.

Meanwhile, I shit down a drain in the concrete floor that is my bed and only home. He cut a trap door in my clown suit, left my raw ass exposed. Every so often, they hose us down. I shiver for days, reek of mildew and sweat. I itch and I ache. And it goes on forever.

So forgive me if I'm fucking depressed.

I look at the corn dog. Only parts of it are green. I sadly thank God I can no longer taste. The last meal I had was cotton candy and gravel, topped with popcorn so stale it broke the last of my teeth.

I think to myself, *should I eat that thing?* There's a part of me that dearly wants to die. Move on. Be free. Reincarnate as a bug, dog, or tree. If there's nothing beyond, just black on black, that's still gotta be way the hell better than this.

I have long given up on Heaven.

But part of me stubbornly wants to live. Knows that something miraculous could happen. A lapse of security. An emotional breakthrough. Revelation. Opportunity. You just never know.

Philosophically speaking, in my dreamiest dreams, I'd love to think I could someday help them see the light. Exorcise this idiotic clown demon. Cut through their psychosis. Transubstantiate the fear. Steer a path toward healing redemption.

But mostly, I just want to rip their fucking throats out, and shit down their necks.

I ain't afraid of you, she says daily, like a mantra.

Oh, but you should be, I think, more and more.

It's the closest to a demon that I will ever get.

And that's how scary clowns are made.

John Skipp is the only *New York Times* bestselling novelist to win a pornographic Oscar for a scene with a singing penis. His splatterpunk novel *The Light At the End* inspired the character of Spike from *Buffy the Vampire Slayer*. His 1989 anthology *Book of the Dead* was the beginning of modern post-Romero zombie fiction. His short fiction with Cody Goodfellow has graced *Hellboy: Oddest Jobs* and the latest *Zombies vs. Robots* collection. Their latest book is *The Last Goddam Hollywood Movie*.

Skipp is also the editor of four massive, encyclopedic anthologies (*Zombies, Demons, Psychos, Werewolves & Shapeshifters*, and editor-in-chief of mainstream-meets-Bizarro publishing imprint **Fungasm Press**. And as filmmaker, he and Andrew Kasch have co-directed the award-winning lactating manboob horror comedy *Stay At Home Dad* and the Slow Poisoner music video *Hot Rod Worm*, with *Robot Chicken* stop motion animator Michael Granberry, in which Skipp also plays the bongos. He lives in L.A.

Howling Through the Keyhole

The stories behind the stories.

"Highballing Through Gehenna"

I ride the train a lot, the northeast corridor Amtrak route between my home in New York City and the family hub in Boston. There is an undercurrent of tension and urgency when you're waiting to board, masses of people jostling for position, instinctively afraid that *the train might leave without them*. The terrain along the route itself is varied, small towns, abandoned, post-apocalyptic mills, anchored boats at seaside marinas and small cities. On one trip, likely inspired by a trackside pizza joint, I saw the rotating disk of the Deformation sailing towards our car. I mean, whammo, the image was conjured whole and furious on the spot. A silent bell-tone indicating *Story Idea* rang in my head and I began to play with it. What if these things attacked the trains on a regular basis? Why would anyone take a train through such dangerous country? Inspired by the empty, red brick structures of the mills, a theme of crumbling civilization introduced itself. I stole more from the actual experience around me, the sights and sounds, the tension before boarding. Next I injected a bit of what my gal likes to call "It's the apocalypse and all you have are the people in this train car, you're in charge." Yikes, scary. Families. Business types. Academics. The only obvious competence lay with the train conductors, who radiated a sense of reliability. The characters stepped forth from this analysis and spoke up quickly to let me know who they were. Even the young telegrapher with rosacea. Not that I identified specific people and worked them into the story, but rather worked to understand the essence of who they were, and let the characters crawl forth from there. Oswego introduced himself unexpectedly and quite firmly as the glue necessary to hold together the slapped together technology and hasty reconstruction of a society on the ropes but not yet down.

Every once in a while a story lands whole in my lap before I even open my laptop and "Highballing Through Gehenna" was that rare beast. It scooped up details and feelings from my travel, passed them through the warped filter of my imagination, and poured out in close to a single sitting. I enjoyed digging up some actual train terminology but had to jigger my geography a bit...in the story they pass the remains of Pittsburgh, I think I originally had them passing Chicago, which made no sense at all when I looked at a map.

Even though I was dying to dig deeper into the details, to explain how Detroit of all places became the last bastion of civilization, to explore the disaster more fully, I held back. The Worth family are *little people* trying to survive something bigger than they are. Something huge. I stuck to what I remembered from my own experiences in the Northridge earthquake, the L.A. riots, Hurricane Sandy. When a giant thing washes over you the world shrinks and big picture considerations take a back seat to caring for who and what is immediately around you. I'm hoping that the ominous ending is seen in this light as well. Young Miri had best enjoy her chicken and waffles and the comfort of electric lights while she can, because the Deformation is coming.

In the story, English teacher and family man Dalton Worth surprises himself and proves his mettle. And of course the doughty Captain Oswego of the Pinkertons has his hand firmly on the tiller. But when I've looked around at the other passengers in the Amtrak Quiet Car on recent trips, I'm glad it's just a story. I think if it were up to us to defend the train against the Deformation, we'd be toast.

–John C. Foster

"We Share the Dark"

Usually, this is the process: I come up with an idea for a story, and then I spend what some might consider a ridiculous amount of time writing notes about said idea, discovering all kinds of neat things about the characters and the world that often don't even end up in the story proper. It's only days and thousands of illegibly scrawled words later that I actually begin writing the work itself.

"We Share the Dark," however, is one of those rare pieces where I sat down with an itch to write and absolutely no idea what I was going to write about. I had a vague image in my mind of a girl and a ghost watching a sunrise or a sunset together from the front porch. I thought it might be a romance between the two, and then Rob walked in. Then I figured Rob was just some awful, sullen ex-boyfriend who would only hang around for a few minutes...but then he kept coming back. And I was like, *Dear God, is this turning into a LOVE TRIANGLE? A love triangle about a medium, a ghost, and a guy who is, for all intents and purposes, a cowboy? How did this happen? Should I make it stop? And just how creepy is TOO creepy for ghost sex these days?*

Despite all this, I like to think it mostly turned out okay.

–Carlie St. George

"The Barham Offramp Playhouse"

"The Barham Offramp Playhouse" came about quite organically, as most of my stories do, with an experience or bit of weird minutiae serving as the dust mote around which ideas and obsessions naturally accreted over a period of years. In point of fact, someone did dump a house up on blocks onto the closed Barham Avenue offramp of 101North in the Cahuenga Pass, sometime in 2008 or 2009. During the two weeks or so it sat on the side of the incredibly busy freeway, it acquired graffiti tags and other signs that it had become not only an accepted part of the landscape but a destination.

I'm fascinated by ruins, and particularly by the new rituals that seem to create themselves in such spaces. Los Angeles is more haunted than any castle or concentration camp in Europe, and filled with more ruins than Rome. Haunted by the ghosts of dreams it took armies to make, and by legions of failed dreamers whose desperation is the defining achievement of their lives. The materialist notion of hauntings, as "psychic residue" or whatever, seemed to dovetail with the actor's imperative to open oneself up to the emotion of the role. They share with the vodun or Santeria practitioner a hunger to be haunted, to be possessed by something Other, if not exactly something higher...

–Cody Goodfellow

"Whisperings Sung Through the Neighborhood of Stilted Sorrows"

"moist, black palimpsestuous layers"

That seems to describe the schizoid, cut-up narrative of the poem. It's a layered collage of dream-like images and associations, and the Freudians would have a field day. It began as snippets of psychosis, tied together by the weaving thread of a dark presence's hunger.

"to whisper from behind closed bedroom doors,
trying to vaccinate the poor child against schizophrenia?"

What is reality to a shattered mind?

–WC Roberts

"Watchtower"

"Watchtower" was born inside a fairy circle not far from Odiorne Point State Park in Rye, New Hampshire. The park used to be an observation outpost during WWII. Remnants of gun emplacements and concrete circles where mortars were positioned facing the Atlantic Ocean to defend against Nazi submarine attack can be found scattered through the brush. It was the juxtaposition of these ruins of war with the naturally occurring—but fancifully named—ring of mushrooms that provided the spore that eventually became "Watchtower".

Those ruins became a secret gateway between worlds, hope in a hopeless situation for my main character as he makes a desperate leap of faith.

While the setting for "Watchtower" evolved from a chance of nature, the characters were born during a writing contest. The challenge was to mix elements of traditional fantasy in a modern military tale. I'm not really a fan of using tropes, so I tried to avoid direct contact with the usual fantasy elements. I don't know if I lived up to the letter of the contest, but I enjoyed writing this piece.

–D.A. D'Amico

"Death and the Maiden"

First time I ever used the word *grave* in a story.

An instinctive identification with the sidekick. Robin, Dr Watson, Tonto, Igor. It's an unhappy story; he doesn't get the girl, his experiment fails and he's doomed from the opening paragraph. Assistants have their uses but shouldn't get ideas above their station.

The Rosencrantz & Guildenstern trope. Minor characters have lives of their own and their own stories to tell. I was pleased with his back story. Did it explain his actions? It was just the way it came out.

The unreliable narrator. I didn't realise until it was nearly finished that Igor murders the child, simply for his own ends, as an experiment, explaining it by saying the child was already marked.

And no remorse. No sympathy for his parents. I don't know that I've ever met a sociopath. Is Igor one? Is it apparent before the end? He has the self-awareness to say he is his own monster, something that has taken a lifetime to create.

–David Barber

"Fat Betty"

Fat Betty is a real cross, located high on the North York moors, and supposedly nicknamed for a local woman, often said to be a nun, who died lost in the wilderness. I first saw it (her?) on a summer evening, when there were storm clouds gathering beyond the valley below. The foreboding weather seemed to be matched by the weirdness of the little cross, with its squat, misshapen form, its crude whitewash, and the soggy offerings of food and coins and wildflowers upon it. It felt a little out of time, a little uncanny, and it made me wonder who the food was for.

Of course, it was going to become a story. The dystopian setting was an odd choice that seemed to grow naturally from that sense of timelessness, and from a sort of sideways reference to the history of the Moorland Crosses in general. Most of them are much bigger than Betty, stone monoliths put up over the centuries as waypoints or landmarks, an attempt to impose a bit of human order on a lawless landscape by people whose lives must have been almost unimaginably harder than those of the walkers who seek out the stones now. It seemed only right that my protagonist be living through similarly dark times.

I've taken some liberties with the geography of the area: Stockdale doesn't exist (to my knowledge), RAF Fylingdales isn't visible from Betty's side of the ridge, and the old railway line above the village of Rosedale is rather more than a short walk away. Greater liberties have been taken with the story, which is invented in total defiance of any actual folklore regarding the cross. There are supposedly "many legends" about Fat Betty, but none of the people or websites I consulted gave more than vague hints, with the occasional outright disappointment. Apparently, the food is left out so that hungry hikers can have a snack en route. How dull.

–Harry Baker

"Stabat Mater"

For me, this story cut a little closer to the bone than most. As "Stabat Mater" originated in Shock Totem's flash fiction contest, I was required to work from a prompt given to all the entrants. Harlan Ellison spoke in an interview of a sort of urban literary myth, in which Hemingway allegedly threw his first book into the sea because "no one should ever read a writer's first novel." ST boss Ken wanted us to write a story based on this theory, but instead of throwing away a first book, we were to focus on throwing away a first child.

A difficult topic to approach, whether one has kids or not. There's a brute power in the very thought of disposing of a baby. But another reason writing "Stabat Mater" affected me strongly was...well, I have only one phobia in the world, and that is of wasps and their flying, stinging brethren. They make me feel like nothing else can. I pictured having a wife, a very pregnant wife, a very pregnant wife kneeling in the leaves with wasps crawling on her...and the shuddering and the writing began. I might have brushed at my arms a few times. And along the way, I hope to have tapped into Nolan's feeling of deeply sad inadequacy.

Arvo Pärt's *Stabat Mater* kept coming into my mind during the seven days we had to write our contest stories. The piece traditionally relates to the sorrows of Mary at the Crucifixion of her son, Christ. I find Pärt's treatment of it particularly dark. The music, scored here for three voices and three stringed instruments, is quiet and raging. I heard Lily in it, yes, but I also heard Nolan.

–Michael Wehunt

"Depresso the Clown"

Everybody needs a cause or two to rally behind, help others, and in the process lend meaning to their lives. And one of mine is to help redeem the Clown as a noble character in the human pantheon.

I really, really like clowns. I always have. To me, they function like the little kid in "The Emperor's New Clothes", pointing out our naked foolishness to the world. Their painted-on smiles and bumbling antics are meant as mirrors to our souls. We're supposed to relate to them. Laugh at ourselves through them.

A keen sense of our own ridiculousness is, I think, a key measure of our wisdom as a species.

The sad clown, in particular, is an icon of beauty: aching with sorrow on the inside, but determined to bring joy to those around them. Just ask the ghost of Federico Fellini.

So it breaks my heart that this valiant tradition, with its roots in honesty, has been unfunhouse-mirrored into a sinister, predatory symbol of hate and fear for the last several generations.

Personally, I blame Tim Curry, Stephen King, and the Chiodo Brothers (*Killer Klowns from Outer Space*). Not saying I don't like what they did. But suddenly, white face and a rubber nose was the equivalent of Hitler's mustache in the "You Must Be A Monster" sweepstakes. An ugly turn of events. And a goddam shame, that I don't think reflects particularly well on our own self-reflection.

Flat-out: we *need* that mirror.

For me, it all came to a head about four years ago, when I got a job closed-captioning TV and motion pictures for the hearing-impaired. And one of my first projects was this incredibly shitty slasher film, with a totally stupid and hateful killer clown killing totally stupid teenagers in totally stupid ways, for some totally stupid reason.

And I went, "ENOUGH! I wanna write some stories where the clowns are the GOOD guys for a fucking change!"

This resulted in an insane screenplay that Cody Goodfellow and I have been sitting on for a while, and are even now scheming into a graphic novel. Probably the funnest thing we've concocted together. I'd tell you more, but that would just be cheating.

In the meantime, I was suddenly inspired to write this story. To me, the image of a clown chained up in a basement pretty much says it all, in terms of what we've done to that once-proud member of our human community.

And with that, I rest my case.

–John Skipp

SILENT Q DESIGN

Silent Q Design was founded in Montreal in 2006 by **Mikio Murakami**. Melding together the use of both realistic templates and surreal imagery, Mikio's artistry proves, at first glance, that a passion for art still is alive, and that no musician, magazine, or venue should suffer from the same bland designs that have been re-hashed over and over.

Mikio's work has been commissioned both locally and internationally, by bands such as **Redemption, Synastry, Starkweather,** and **Epocholypse.** *Shock Totem #3* was his first book design project.

For more info, visit **www.silentqdesign.net.**

ALSO AVAILABLE FROM SHOCK TOTEM PUBLICATIONS

CURIOUS TALES *of the* MACABRE *and* TWISTED
SHOCK TOTEM

T.L. Morganfield
Kurt Newton • Don D'Ammassa
Jennifer Pelland • David Niall Wilson
Interviews with John Skipp, William Ollie, and Alan Robert

SHOCK TOTEM MAGAZINE
Issue #1 – July 2009

AVAILABLE NOW IN PRINT AND DIGITAL FORMATS
www.SHOCKTOTEM.com

ALSO AVAILABLE FROM SHOCK TOTEM PUBLICATIONS

CURIOUS TALES *of the* MACABRE *and* TWISTED
SHOCK TOTEM

Leslianne Wilder
Ricardo Bare • Cate Gardner
Vincent Pendergast • David Jack Bell
Grá Linnaea & Sarah Dunn
A conversation with James Newman • Nonfiction by Mercedes M. Yardley

SHOCK TOTEM MAGAZINE
Issue #2 – July 2010
AVAILABLE NOW IN PRINT AND DIGITAL FORMATS
www.SHOCKTOTEM.com

ALSO AVAILABLE FROM SHOCK TOTEM PUBLICATIONS

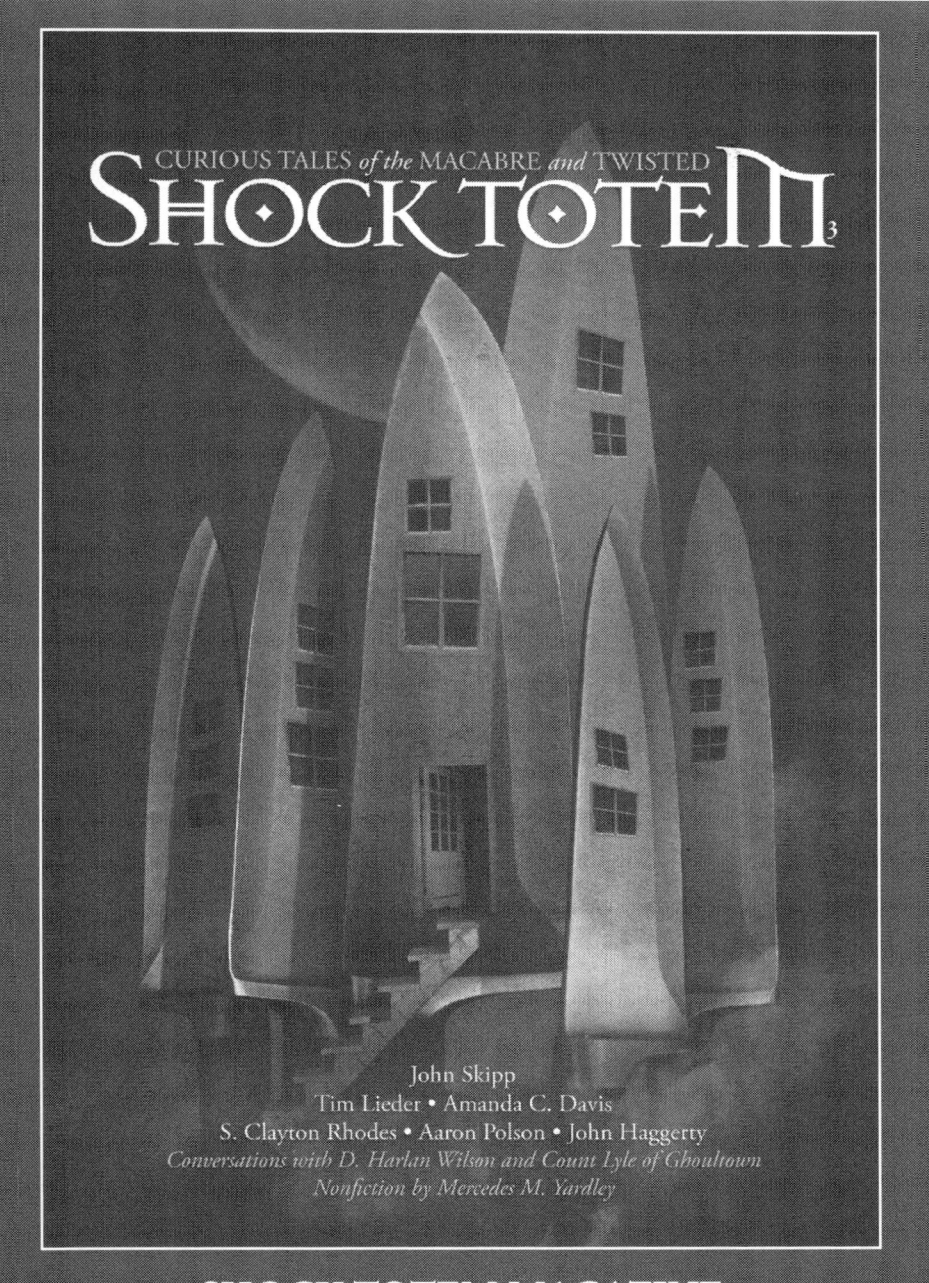

CURIOUS TALES *of the* MACABRE *and* TWISTED

SHOCK TOTEM 3

John Skipp
Tim Lieder • Amanda C. Davis
S. Clayton Rhodes • Aaron Polson • John Haggerty
Conversations with D. Harlan Wilson and Count Lyle of Ghoultown
Nonfiction by Mercedes M. Yardley

SHOCK TOTEM MAGAZINE
Issue #3 – January 2011
AVAILABLE NOW IN PRINT AND DIGITAL FORMATS
www.SHOCKTOTEM.com

ALSO AVAILABLE FROM SHOCK TOTEM PUBLICATIONS

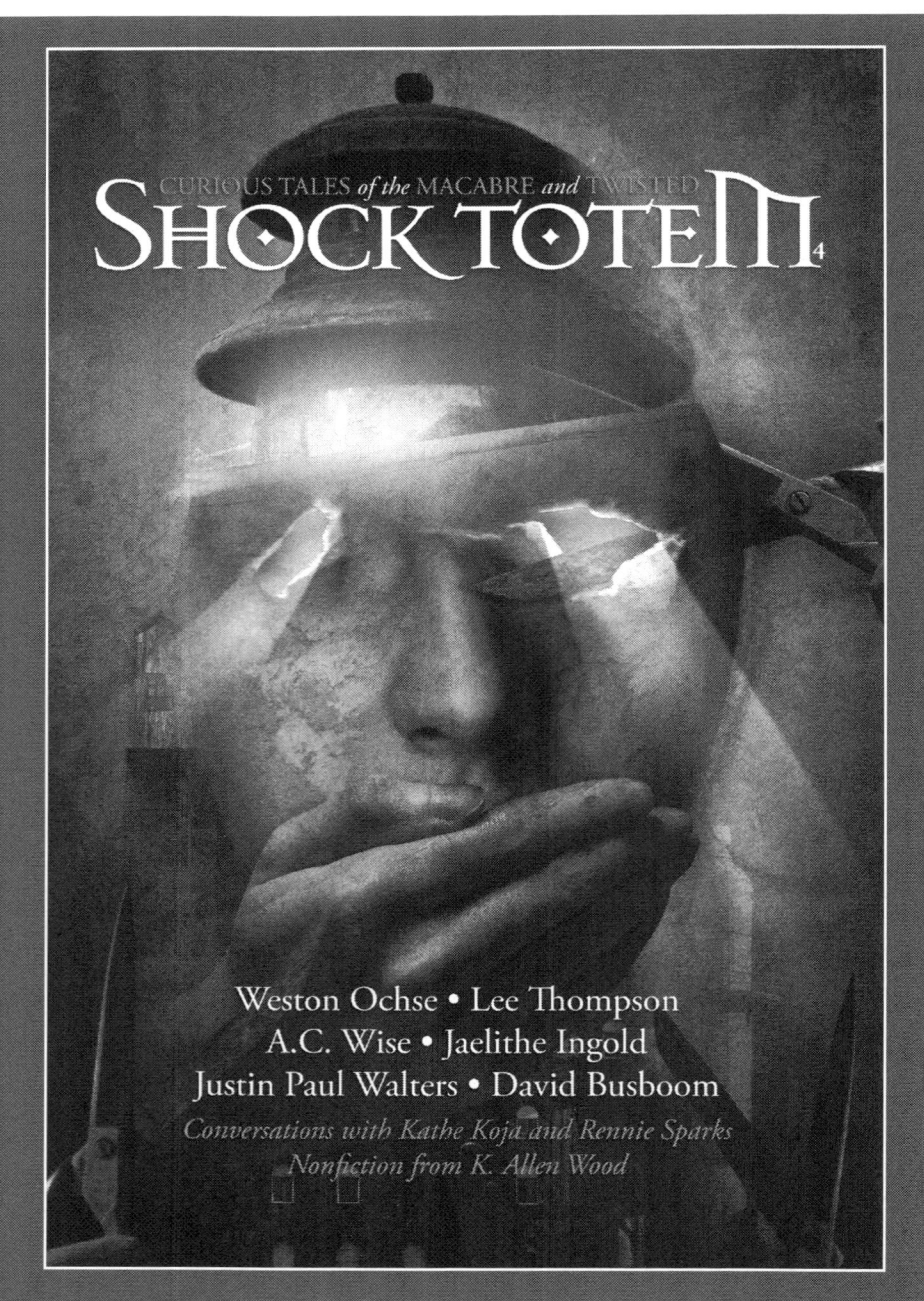

CURIOUS TALES *of the* **MACABRE** *and* **TWISTED**
SHOCK TOTEM 4

Weston Ochse • Lee Thompson
A.C. Wise • Jaelithe Ingold
Justin Paul Walters • David Busboom
Conversations with Kathe Koja and Rennie Sparks
Nonfiction from K. Allen Wood

SHOCK TOTEM MAGAZINE
Issue #4 – July 2011
AVAILABLE NOW IN PRINT AND DIGITAL FORMATS
www.SHOCKTOTEM.com

ALSO AVAILABLE FROM SHOCK TOTEM PUBLICATIONS

HOLIDAY TALES *of the* MACABRE *and* TWISTED 2011
SHOCK TOTEM

K. Allen Wood • Mercedes M. Yardley • Kevin J. Anderson
Robert J. Duperre • John Boden • Ryan Bridger
Nick Contor • Sarah Gomes

Holiday Recollections from Jack Ketchum, Mark Allan Gunnells, Lee Thompson, Leslianne Wilder, Jennifer Pelland, Nick Cato and More...

SHOCK TOTEM MAGAZINE
Special Holiday Issue – November 2011
AVAILABLE NOW IN DIGITAL FORMAT
www.SHOCKTOTEM.com

ALSO AVAILABLE FROM SHOCK TOTEM PUBLICATIONS

CURIOUS TALES *of the* MACABRE *and* TWISTED

SHOCK TOTEM 5

Ari Marmell · Darrell Schweitzer
Kurt Newton · Joe Mirabello · Sean Eads
Mckenzie Larsen · Jaelithe Ingold
Conversations with Jack Ketchum · Nonfiction from Nick Contor

SHOCK TOTEM MAGAZINE
Issue #5 – July 2012
AVAILABLE NOW IN PRINT AND DIGITAL FORMATS
www.SHOCKTOTEM.com

ALSO AVAILABLE FROM SHOCK TOTEM PUBLICATIONS

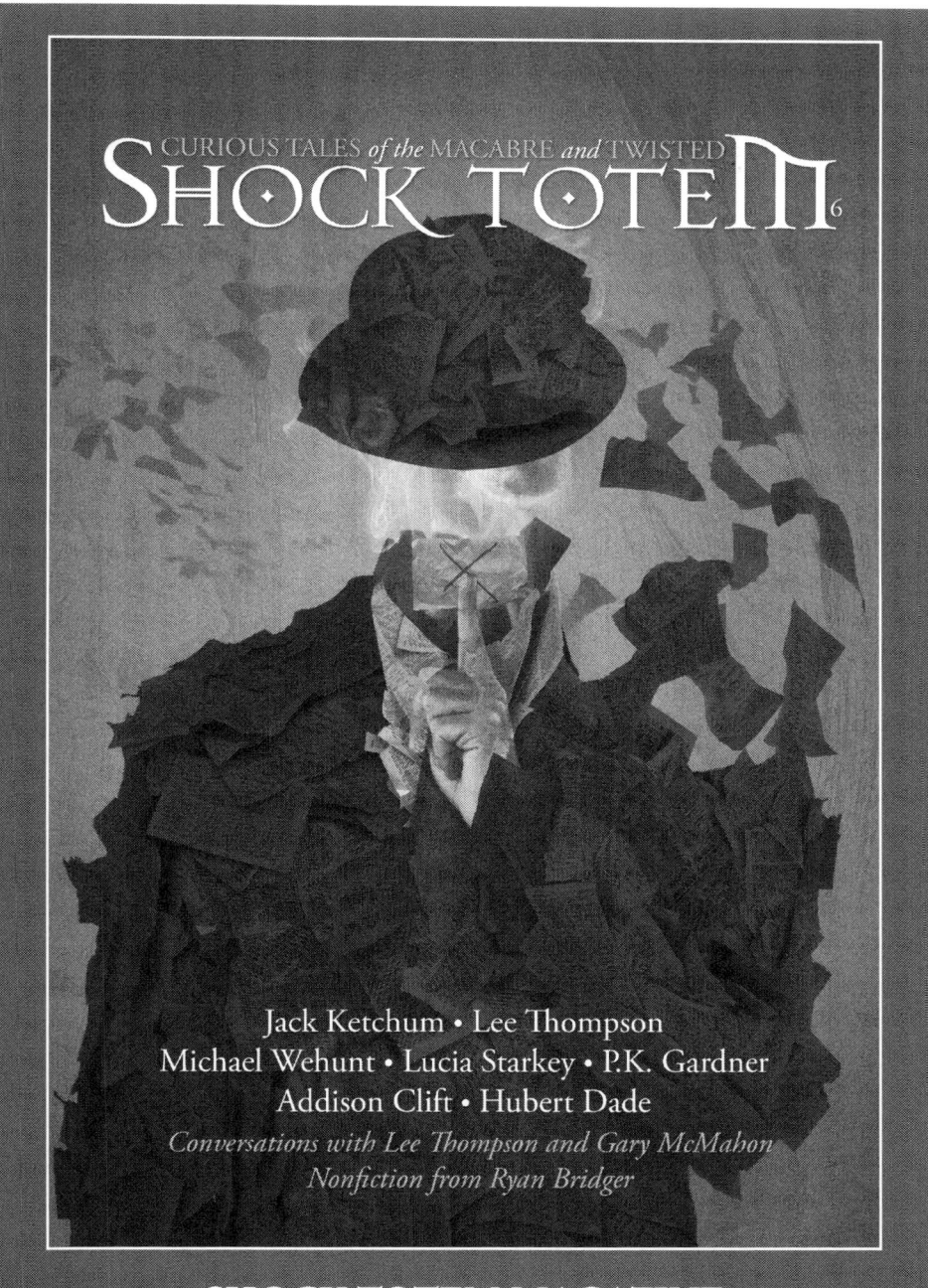

CURIOUS TALES *of the* MACABRE *and* TWISTED
SHOCK TOTEM ₆

Jack Ketchum • Lee Thompson
Michael Wehunt • Lucia Starkey • P.K. Gardner
Addison Clift • Hubert Dade
Conversations with Lee Thompson and Gary McMahon
Nonfiction from Ryan Bridger

SHOCK TOTEM MAGAZINE
Issue #6 – January 2013
AVAILABLE NOW IN PRINT AND DIGITAL FORMATS
www.SHOCKTOTEM.com

ALSO AVAILABLE FROM SHOCK TOTEM PUBLICATIONS

CURIOUS TALES *of the* MACABRE *and* TWISTED
SHOCK TOTEM

William F. Nolan • S. Clayton Rhodes
Amberle L. Husbands • Kristi DeMeester • M. Bennardo
Damien Angelica Walters • Victoria Jakes
Conversations with Laird Barron and Violet LeVoit
Nonfiction from Kurt Newton

SHOCK TOTEM MAGAZINE
Issue #7 – July 2013
AVAILABLE NOW IN PRINT AND DIGITAL FORMATS
www.SHOCKTOTEM.com

ALSO AVAILABLE FROM SHOCK TOTEM PUBLICATIONS

"*Ugly As Sin*...is the most jaundiced indictment possible of the corrupted soul of celebrity culture...its feeders and especially its fed." —Brian Hodge

UGLY AS SIN

A NOVEL OF WHITE-TRASH NOIR BY

JAMES NEWMAN

UGLY AS SIN
JAMES NEWMAN
AVAILABLE NOW IN PRINT AND DIGITAL FORMATS
www.SHOCKTOTEM.com

ALSO AVAILABLE FROM SHOCK TOTEM PUBLICATIONS

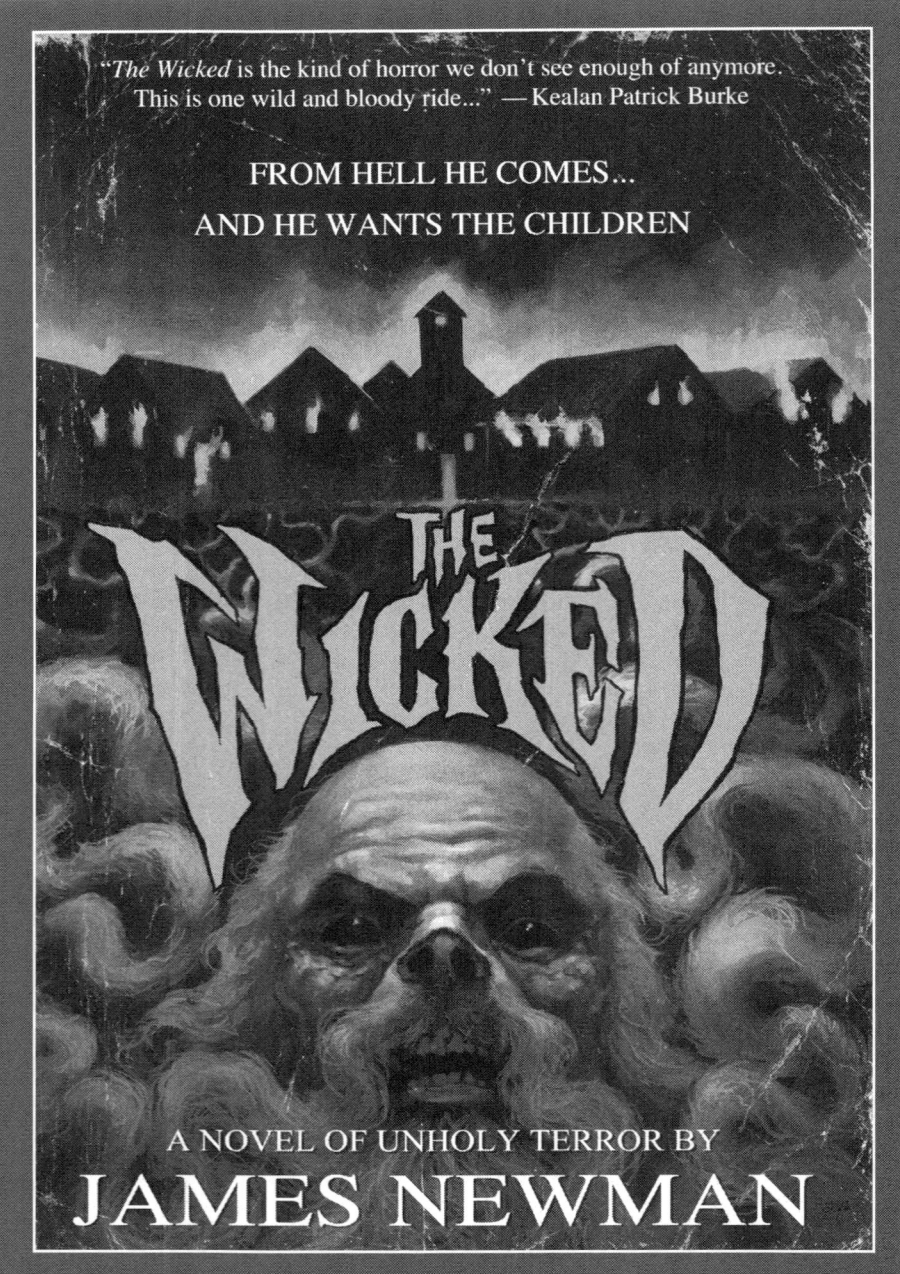

"*The Wicked* is the kind of horror we don't see enough of anymore. This is one wild and bloody ride..." —Kealan Patrick Burke

FROM HELL HE COMES...
AND HE WANTS THE CHILDREN

THE WICKED

A NOVEL OF UNHOLY TERROR BY
JAMES NEWMAN

THE WICKED
JAMES NEWMAN
AVAILABLE NOW IN PRINT AND DIGITAL FORMATS
www.SHOCKTOTEM.com

ALSO AVAILABLE FROM SHOCK TOTEM PUBLICATIONS

MERCEDES M. YARDLEY

"Beautiful Sorrows... delicate prose with devastating impact. Mercedes Yardley is a female Joe Hill..." —F. Paul Wilson

BEAUTIFUL SORROWS
MERCEDES M. YARDLEY
AVAILABLE NOW IN PRINT AND DIGITAL FORMATS
www.SHOCKTOTEM.com

Find Us Online

http://www.shocktotem.com
http://www.twitter.com/shocktotem
http://www.facebook.com/shocktotem
http://www.youtube.com/shocktotemmag

Shock Totem Submission Guidelines

What We Want: We consider original, unpublished stories within the confines of dark fantasy and horror—mystery, suspense, supernatural, morbid humor, fantasy, etc. Stories must have a clear horror element.

We are interested in tightly woven flash fiction, 1,000 words or less, and microfiction, 200 words or less.

We are interested in dark poetry on a limited basis.

We want well-researched and emotionally compelling nonfiction about real horrors—disease, poverty, addiction, etc. We will also consider work on other, relative subjects within the confines of dark fantasy and horror.

What We Do Not Want: We're not interested in hard science fiction, epic fantasy (swords and sorcery), splatterporn (blood and guts and little more), or clichéd plots. Clichéd *themes* are okay. No fan fiction.

What We Will Consider: Reprints not published within the last 12 months. Author must retain all applicable rights.

Average Response Time: 2 months.

Payment Rates: We pay 5 cents per word for original, unpublished fiction. We pay 2 cents per word for reprints. There is a $250 cap on all accepted pieces.

Rights: For previously unpublished work we claim First North American Serial Rights and First Electronic World Rights (not to include Internet use) for a period of one year. After which all rights revert to the author.

For previously published work we claim Exclusive Reprint Rights and Exclusive Electronic World Reprint Rights (not to include Internet use) for a period of six months. After which all rights revert to the author.

For more detailed information, please visit us at
www.shocktotem.com

Copyright © 2014 by Shock Totem Publications, LLC.

Made in the USA
Charleston, SC
04 June 2014